Beautiful Sorrows

ALSO BY MERCEDES M. YARDLEY

Darling
Little Dead Red
Pretty Little Dead Girls
Nameless: The Darkness Comes
Detritus In Love (with John Boden)
Apocalyptic Montessa and Nuclear Lulu: A Tale of Atomic Love

Beautiful ☆ Sorrows

Mercedes M. Yardley

All stories are original to this collection unless otherwise noted:

"The Boy Who Hangs the Stars" *Neverlands and Otherwheres* (2008)
"Pixies Don't Get Names" *Reflection's Edge* (2008)
"Show Your Bones" *The Vestal Review* (2008), *The Shine Journal* (2008)
"The ABCs of Murder" *On the Premises* (2009)
"The Container of Sorrows" *The Pedestal Magazine* (2009)
"Flat, Flat World" *Silverthought* (2009)
"Life" *Abandoned Towers* (2009)
"She Called Him Sky" (as "Flowers") *BluePrintReview* (2009)
"Broken" *Wigleaf* (2010)
"Blossom Bones" *The Binnacle* (2010/2011)
"The Container of Sorrows" *The Gate: 13 Dark and Odd Tales* (2010)
"Heartless" *Shock Totem: Holiday Tales of the Macabre and Twisted* (2011)
"Stars" *Best New Writing 2012* (2012)
"Black Mary" *The Gate 2: 13 Tales of Isolation and Despair* (2012)

www.mercedesmyardley.com

For Mein. All of you.

✬✬ TABLE OF CONTENTS ✬✬

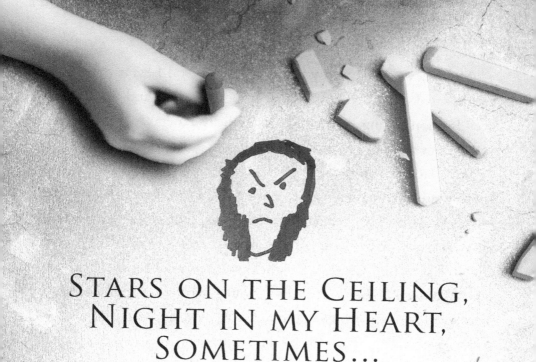

STARS ON THE CEILING, NIGHT IN MY HEART, SOMETIMES...

by John Boden

Being asked to craft an introduction is...can be...quite intimidating. Steeped in a worry that readers and peers will dispense it as just friend-lofting fluff and not at all truthful in its desire to guide your hand to the waiting paw of said author. Fear of disservice looms tall and bitter.

I have known Mercedes M. Yardley, or My Dearest M, as I have called her in messages and text, for around thirteen years. Give or take, time is an old rubber band after so long, cracking and unreliable in how far it can be pulled before snapping. A baker's dozen of years equals a lifetime in the writing world. Genres have imploded or burned bright as suns. Big names wither like sick limbs and curl in dark corners while fresh faces and names run up and down the flagpoles with fever.

Mercedes came into my life as did the reason I even write now, via the mad dream of Ken Allen Wood. That cat and I have been friends a long, long time, haunters of heavy metal message boards and covens for those with CD.[1]

Ken had a bee in his bonnet about wanting to start an old school horror fiction kinda magazine. He recruited me along with our pal, Nick Contor and we had a few "other guys" that came and went but we eventually got a debut issue together after a year of hard work and web jousting. One of the stories we accepted for the first issue was "Murder For Beginners" by a young woman named Mercedes Yardley. The issue dropped and her story was a standout in reviews and tongue wagging and I....*think*...that led to Ken asking her to join the crew. She did and we worked together, until the press shut its creaking doors after 9 issues... rising from the mossy earth and recruiting Chad Lutzke to fill in for the reclusive Nick and help us sling together a 10th issue later. All of that to say, Mercedes is a dear friend...an amazing mother and wife and one of the most kind-hearted souls I have ever encountered. And it has made me so very proud to watch her continue to blaze her path with her wholly original brand of fiction.

She also pens absolute magic. Dark. Lyrical. Whimsical. Brutal. That's My Dearest M. to the letter.

Beautiful Sorrows was her debut collection, originally released in September of 2012 at Killercon in Las Vegas. The first and last time I ever spent time in real space with Mercedes. A wild weekend of diner food and laughter and books and dreams and more laughter. The book trucked along until *Shock Totem* folded and it went to Jason

---

1   Many moons ago, music was captured and trafficked primarily on silvery plastic circles, madness, I know.

Sizemore at Apex Publishing, and I lost track after that, busy pursuing my own paths in the dark forests of fiction. I am thrilled to see a newer generation get a fresh look at this collection. It is overdue.

There were 27 stories in this book (I'm looking at my original edition hardback, counting on my fingers) and four new ones added to this version. I can attest to the power it contains with the fact that the opening tale, BROKEN, is exactly two sentences long and has been burned into my memory since I first read it in the vendor suite of that hotel in Vegas, all those years ago. Simple and scalpel sharp as the best words alway are. Now, to be transparent, I have not read this book in a number of years and cannot assign titles to conceits readily, but I do recall that the pages are swimming with beasts, magical and mortal. There be witches in here, and villains, lonely souls, and wise children as well as gorgeous night skies and dreary dark days. Time stands still and trudges on hearts and minds and fingers. Like a child's bedroom at night, with stars on the ceiling and night in their heart...innocent terror and cuddly sadness. Yet, there is always...well, *usually* some kind of hope, even if nestled in the frothy corner of that gnashing little mouth of the thing in the darkness. Her writing is furiously personal and that is the rock that cuts the edge, sometimes smooth sometimes not, but eager to wound. This is a promise.

I have always felt that the work of Mercedes Yardley is carved from the same tonal stone as Laughton's film, *Night of the Hunter*. I still feel that way. I don't know if she has ever read Davis Grubb's novel or stories but there is a kinship there in the convoluted simplicity of word stitchery.

I feel confident that hers will be a name slung about in the future, in much the way we bandy about our old influential lot...Bradbury,

11

Margaret St. Clair, King, Rice…whomever peoples *your* list, it is my sincerest hope that Yardley will appear on it in a future edition. That a ghostly finger shall scrawl it on that place in your heart where you fan influential flames and joy. She deserves that place. Very much so.

Yours from my corner of the basement,
John Boden

BROKEN

The dried twigs cracking under her feet broke exactly like the small bones of children. She wished she didn't know that.

BLACK MARY

The other girl, she has eyes like oil. They're dark and black and slick. They widen like holes and one day they'll swallow me completely.

I tell her this. She smiles, just a little.

"Maybe."

I go outside to drag some heavy wood to the house. I wear a large pair of men's boots that I tie as tightly as I can, but I still step out of them. I'm not allowed to have a pair that fits.

The wood is running low and this worries me. The wolves howl in the freezing night, venturing from the forest that looms on the edge of the fields. The dank little house doesn't have windows that fully shut. There's no way to keep the wind out.

"If you bring me an axe, I'll chop my own wood," I had told him on Tuesday. At least he had mentioned it was Tuesday. I stood there in bare feet, hugging my arms around my torn dress. "You won't have to do anything. I'll do all the work for you."

He hit me then, once, hard enough that it knocked me to the ground and I couldn't get up right away. Black Mary crouched over me like a cat, hissing at him. He didn't seem to notice her.

Later he took me to his bed, gently rubbing my freezing arms and legs. The black-haired girl stood in the doorway, silently. I met her eyes over his greasy shoulder.

"Little girls aren't meant to use axes, honey," he said. "What if you hurt yourself? Nobody is here to help you, not for miles. It isn't safe. Do you understand?"

I wanted to tell him that I would be careful, that I was almost eleven years old, but I only nodded, my hands clasped between my knees.

"Tell ya what I'll do. I'll bring in wood when I come, okay? Lots of it. Will that make you happy?"

I nodded, and the gentle caress on my arm turned into something different. The girl turned away and I squeezed my eyes shut.

That was two days ago. Now the black-eyed girl stands behind me, brushing my hair. "He wears a wedding ring," she said. "That means he has a wife. Maybe some kids. Maybe his kids are the same age you are."

I turn my head to the side and throw up. "Sorry," I say, and wipe my mouth with the back of my hand.

She steps in front of me and crouches until we're eye level. "Don't you ever apologize to me, get it? I'm your friend. I love you—real love—nothing like what *he* says love is." Her eyes burn, scorch. Fire rushing across oil. "I'd like to kill him."

"You wouldn't!"

Black Mary is fierce. "I would. He knows it. Why doesn't he leave an axe here, huh? Because he knows I'll kill him one day. I'll take that axe and swipe at his head when he isn't looking. Or even when he *is.* Either way."

I back up a little.

She snorts.

"What, I'm too harsh for you? Are you scared, sweet little thing?" She stands up, tossing her hair back. "This is why he takes you, you know. You, and not me. Because you give in. Because you're so good and quiet, and men love little girls who are quiet. Me?" She shrugs. "Nobody loves me. Not anymore."

She turns and walks away. It hurts me to see her go, but I have other things to tend to. I still have bruises, inside and out. I still have the nightmares.

Black Mary has been gone for several days. I look for her on the horizon, but there isn't anything besides fields of weeds. The food is almost gone. I'm hungry and sick and almost want the man to come again so that I can have something to eat. Almost.

"That's what he wants, you know," Black Mary says to me. She's sitting on a large rock out in the field. Her pointed nose and shiny hair reminds me of a crow. A raven. Something that could simply fly away.

"Why did you come back?" I ask her.

"Didn't you miss me?" She tilts her head like a bird. I wonder if she sheds her skin at night and there are feathers underneath.

"Of course I missed you. I missed you so much. But weren't you free? Didn't you get away? Why would you come back?"

She reaches for my hand but I pull it away.

"Do you remember your mother?"

I freeze. "Why?"

My mother wore yellow dresses and grew lavender in the front yard. Her eyes were brown, like mine. Or maybe they were blue.

"Do you think she's out there looking for you?"

I sit down, my back against the rock. My stomach is hurting.

"Do you think your mother is still looking?" She isn't letting the question go unanswered.

I want to think so. But it's been so long. She probably gave up by now. I wipe my face with my sleeve.

"Know what I think?"

I shake my head.

She slides off the rock and grabs my wrists. She's careful of the bruises, as always. "I think moms never stop looking for their kids. Not ever. No matter how long they've been gone."

"I don't look the same anymore."

"No, you don't. You've grown a lot in the last few years."

"What if she doesn't recognize me?"

"What if she does?"

I cough and the black-eyed girl draws away. "Come on. We need to get you inside. You're getting sick and you remember what that's like. Maybe when he comes back, he'll bring more wood."

He doesn't. He doesn't bring much food, either, just a cheeseburger from a fast food place and a shopping bag full of apples.

"Is...is there anything else?" I ask, and I pay for it.

The girl with the black hair helps me up and stands behind me while I wash the blood from my dress. I meet her eyes in the mirror.

"Something's wrong, did you notice?" Her arms are folded across her chest. "See how he's pacing like that? Be careful."

He barks for me and I come.

The girl is right. Something's wrong.

"Have you been out of this house, Mary?" he demands.

My name isn't Mary. I told him that once, but he didn't care. We're all Mary here.

"Yes, sir. Just to the field and the wood pile."

"No farther?"

"No, sir." There isn't anywhere else to go. Nothing but fields and rocks and animals that run through the grass.

He leans close, his face red and his eyes wild.

I flinch and this seems to make him angrier.

"You afraid of me, girl?"

I don't know what to say.

He raises his fist.

The girl with the black hair stands behind him, her eyes huge. They're leaking oil.

I'm still staring at her when he hits me. A few more blows and I squeal, "How come you only hurt me and not Black Mary?" The second I say it, I wish I could take it back. "I'm sorry, I'm sorry," I tell her, but she crouches in the corner, her hands over her ears, away from me.

The man demands to know if I love him. I try to say no. I try to say yes. My mouth is too swollen to work properly. The man stares at me in a new way and leaves. He's never left before morning. Even though I'm grateful, my stomach twists and I'm afraid.

A new girl arrives with the sunrise. She's younger than I am. She has curly red hair and freckles. Like me, she's in a torn dress. Like me, her feet are bare.

"Who are you?" I ask. It hurts to move my jaw.

"This is Red Mary."

The girl with the black hair has bruises around her eyes. Her

19

long hair has been cut, shaggy and boyish, like mine. She has displeased him.

"What happened to you?" I want to ask, but I'm afraid that she'll tell me. He found her. He went to her. I pointed her out and she isn't safe anymore.

Red Mary speaks. Her voice is tremulous, soft like tiny bells. "He asked me if I liked toys. He said that we could play games."

I turn and look at her. Seize her arm, yank up her sleeve. Her skin is white, without marks in the shape of his fingers. Her eyes are scared but not horrified. Not yet.

"He said that to me," I tell her. I grab her hand. She grabs back.

"He said that to me, too." Black Mary's voice has changed. It sounds tired, more like mine. Like she's given up.

I'm not giving up. Not if we can save Red Mary.

"We need to go," I say.

The girls look at me.

I swallow hard. "We need to go."

"Go?" Red Mary asks. She's so trusting. She'd holding onto a gray stuffed bunny that I haven't noticed before. I had one just like it when I was little.

"He'll hurt you," I tell her. "He'll keep you here and do...horrible things."

She starts to tremble. "What kind of things?"

My breath hitches and I can't talk for a minute. I catch Black Mary's eye. One is starting to swell shut, but she still tries to smile at me.

"If he catches you, he'll kill you," Black Mary says. "You know that he will."

I know.

I don't have anything to take with me except the apples. I shove my feet into the too-big boots and stuff them with newspaper. It had snowed during the night. I wish that I had a coat.

"Now we run," I say, and take Red Mary by the hand. My muscles ache and new cuts from last night open up. But we keep moving.

"I'm tired," Red Mary says after a few hours. "I want to go back."

I shake my head. "You don't."

Black Mary slogs through the snow beside me. She isn't even breathing heavy.

"Do you remember," Black Mary says, "when we tried to run away before? You were little, just like Red Mary. We got about this far and then you turned back."

I'm shocked. "Did I? Why would I do that?"

She shrugs. "You didn't know any better. You didn't know what he was like, then."

My sides hurt. My feet are blistered, but I know that if I stop, he'll catch me. There was something wrong last night, something in his eyes that makes my mouth go dry.

"He's in trouble. Maybe somebody knows. Or maybe," Black Mary says, blood running from the corner of her mouth, "you're too old."

"What do you mean, too old?"

"You know what I mean."

The snow starts to fall again. The cough from earlier deepens in my lungs.

"Are you going to die?" Red Mary asks. She's skipping through the snow, not seeming to feel the cold. Her red hair is the only splash of color I see.

"That's not a nice thing to ask," Black Mary scolds. Her hair is back to its long, shiny length, her black eyes healed.

"But is she? Are you?" Red Mary turns to me.

I don't know what to say.

Black Mary lies down in the snow. "Maybe I'll just wait here until he finds me. Oh, he's going to be so *mad*." Her eyes glitter. "Don't you think he'll be *mad?*"

"You need to stand up," I tell her, and pull at her arm. Suddenly I realize that she is the one who is standing. I'm lying in a snowdrift, my hair blowing over my face. I had almost fallen asleep.

"Run," Black Mary says, and Red Mary echoes her. "Run."

It's getting dark now. I scramble to my knees and crawl through the snow, not strong enough to run. At least the burning pain of freezing to death makes me think of something other than my bruises.

There's a light. It's small and beautiful. I ask the girls if they see it.

"What light?" Black Mary asks, and she falls.

"I'm cold," Red Mary whispers, and she also falls.

I try to drag Red Mary but I only get a few feet. She's too heavy. I'm too cold.

"I'll get help," I say, but they don't answer.

The light is coming from a window in a small house on the edge of a field. It looks like it might be painted yellow. I think my mom's house was yellow.

"It was, when you were younger," Black Mary says. She's crawling through the snow with me.

"Feeling better?" I ask her.

Her eyes are like ice. "No."

We make it to the porch. I'm on my knees, hesitating. Black Mary puts her hand on my shoulder.

"We can always go back if you want."

I knock on the door. The bones in my hands feel like they'll shatter from the cold.

A shadow moves in the window. I want to scream, and I do. Shadows hit and twist and bite. Shadows hurt you from the inside out.

The shadow opens the door. It is a woman. She looks at me and her hand goes to her mouth.

"Oh my goodness. Oh no," she says. She calls over her shoulder for a blanket and some hot chocolate and the police. She looks back at me, reaching out with both hands. She touches my skin and we both draw back.

"Are you alone, sweetheart?"

Black Mary sweeps past her into the house. Red Mary sits on the porch, sucking her thumb.

"You're too old to do that," I tell her. I look back at the woman.

"My mom had a yellow house, I think. Do you know my mom?"

The blanket arrives. She spreads it out and I gingerly step into it, my eyes on Black Mary. She nods, and I let the woman wrap it around me and lead me inside.

"What's your name, sweetie?" The woman is all eyes, taking in my tattered dress and ratted hair, the bruises and dried blood. I want to say that she should check on Red Mary, but the little girl seems happy. She seems okay.

My name. It's been too long. I scribbled it on the page of a book once, but he threw all of the books away one day when he was angry.

"I can't remember. I'm just one of the Marys."

The woman's voice was patient, carefully so. "One of the Marys? Which one?"

A man enters the room, saying something about the police being on their way. I see him and shrink back. He is big and tall and his hands could wrap around my throat so easily. The man looks like he wants to say something, but he only uses his big hands to pass a mug to the woman and steps away.

"Which Mary?" the woman asks again. Her eyes are soft. She shows me that the mug is full of hot cocoa.

"I don't know. Maybe White Mary. Do you think my mom will remember me?"

Red Mary taps the woman on her thigh. "We're all Mary here," she tells her, but the woman doesn't look at her. Not once. She doesn't even seem to notice.

FLAT, FLAT WORLD

"Sometimes I just want to take a step backward off the flat, flat world," the girl said to no one in particular. She was alone, lying under the newly shorn tree that had once been so glorious. It was broken now, like everything else. It had no glitter. The tree shook its limbs valiantly and only a few dead leaves fell into the girl's hair. The tree hung its branches low. It had meant to tremble flowers.

The girl didn't notice the dead leaves, or the creeping spider that had landed in her hair as well. She was busy staring into nothing. The spider perched in her hair, fancying itself a butterfly. This wasn't to be so.

The girl rolled onto her back, sighing as she noticed the blue piece of chewing gum stuck to the tree's bark. "They've gotten you, too," she said, and the tree nodded, although neither had any idea who "they" were or what, exactly, they had done.

The girl stood up then, which was unfortunate because the spider chose at that moment to leap from her hair, flapping his eight legs furiously as a butterfly would. The wind sent it spiraling into the chewing gum, still faintly sticky, and three of its legs were held fast. It dangled and struggled and pulled, then hung limply. It contemplated its fate, wondering if it had the courage to pull the three legs off in order to save the other five.

The tree was merciful. It slapped a long branch against the gum. The girl noticed none of this, just concentrated on placing one foot in front of the other as she walked away. Her body left no imprint in the grass where she had been lying and her footsteps didn't make a sound.

Nobody saw her as she floated by, brown leaves falling from her hair.

Once again, the tree wished for flowers.

She fell asleep while on the floor of her apartment, watching for a mouse to pop out of the hole in the baseboard. In truth there was no mouse, and she knew this, but perhaps if she hoped with enough fervor one would appear.

In her dream, a flood came and swept her away. She watched her hair sway like seaweed, in its element like it belonged to a nymph. She turned to face herself and smiled.

"I don't want to surface," she said, and promptly drowned.

The tide pulled her along, her fingers loose and relaxed, her curious dead eyes the same color as the sea. She briefly worried that the floating, swirling white dress she was wearing had pushed up and was exposing too much pale thigh, but dismissed the thought easily. The sea can be a gentle lover when it wishes, and really, what's a little leg? She felt envious watching her empty body spin lazily in the current.

Well, I don't want to surface, either, she thought. But she did surface, waking up cold and stiff on her kitchen floor. The mouse still hadn't been wished into being, despite how many crackers she had placed in front of the hole. Maybe tonight she would learn to pray.

She slipped on a soft robe and sank down into the chair at the vanity. The hair pins made a clinking sound as she pulled them from her hair and tossed them into a bowl before picking up her brush. She had scarcely brushed a stroke when her eyes caught somebody else's in the mirror.

"It's you," she said.

"It's me."

He took the brush out of her hand and went to work on her hair. She sat quietly while he did this, wondering vaguely if he had simply walked through the wall as he usually did.

"Yes," he said.

"I thought so."

Her hair began to shine. The leaves and cobwebs fell out of it and hit the floor with the sound of chimes. She thought of stars.

"I might have a mouse," she said.

"Yes," he said again.

He came by every so often, leaning against the wall, looking at the palms of his hands, not acknowledging her before leaving. She never remembered what he looked like when he was gone. She had never asked his name.

"It doesn't matter," he said.

No, it didn't.

He set the silver brush down and pulled her to her feet. Putting one hand on the back of her head, he kissed her.

She returned the kiss dutifully and without passion. Her hands rested on either side of his face, pressing against the solid bone beneath his skin. She traced the features of his skull with her fingers, and her skin shimmered and passed through like fog.

The girl took a step back in vague surprise. He took a deep breath, and a swirl of vapor left her body and passed through his lips, down into his lungs. She felt that part of herself disappear.

She dropped her transparent fingers from his face. "I don't like that you're solid and I'm not."

The man watched her with quiet eyes. "You didn't want to surface," he said.

Oh. That's right. Somehow she had forgotten.

Her eyebrows worked as she frowned. "But I don't want to disappear entirely," she said. She bit her lip, looking at the ground. "I want to still be here."

"Do you?"

Did she?

Her robe was too thin. She clutched at it, realized her hand was trembling. Her eyes met his, and she saw herself there.

"I don't know," she said honestly. Her fingers worried the soft fabric. It was flimsy and yielding. She wanted to be dressed in crisp leaves and curls of bark. She wanted to sway under the sky. She reached out and felt the fabric of his shirt between her fingers. It was stiffer, more substantial. She imagined taking it and wrapping it around her body. She looked away in case he could see what she was thinking.

"I always know what you're thinking."

She ran her fingers down his sleeves, slid her hands inside. There was no warmth there. No coolness. Nothing at all.

"You don't really exist," she told him. His lips turned up slightly at the corners, but then it was gone. She took a step closer. "You are a figment of my imagination." She wanted to bite the underside of his jaw to prove he wasn't really there, but she stopped herself.

His voice, as always, held no emotion. "Does thinking this make you feel better?"

She didn't know.

She turned from him and looked out of the window. The tree

from earlier waved its branches at her happily. She timidly waved back. The tree caught a glimpse of the man behind her and suddenly snapped to attention. It held itself straight and proud, no leaf daring to drift from its branches.

The man stepped closer and pinned her arms to her sides. His mouth was close to her ear.

"I am more real than you are," he said. His breath made wisps of her hair flutter. She was not certain her breath could do the same.

She thought about this. "Then I must not be very real at all." This thought didn't seem unpleasant.

He released her, started walking away. "You are as real as you want to be," he said. He turned and smiled at her then, and it was heartbreakingly lovely. "It's your choice, you know."

Her choice. Yes, she thought she liked that.

The man was fading, and soon there would be nothing left. She took a small step forward.

"I...think I want to come with you." Her voice already sounded like the wind through the trees. "I want to see where you go. I want to see what you know."

He held out his hand. She could barely see the outline of it. "Come, then," he said. She reached for it, and this time his fingers felt warm and strong and substantial as they curled around hers.

Her robe collapsed into a silken pool on the ground. It was exactly right. Outside, the tree bowed deeply. Your majesty. Your majesty.

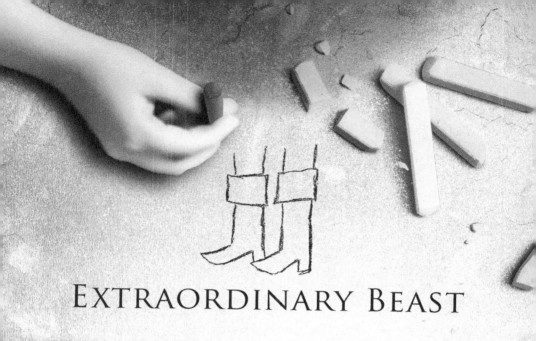

EXTRAORDINARY BEAST

He made her anxious. He made her anxious.

A tall, thin thing, a modern day Spring-Heeled Jack. His voice, when he spoke, was all lies and promises, sexy and deep, chartreuse and nuance and Lily of the Valley.

She should go to him, should ask his name although he would never tell. The sound of his boots against the gravel was glory. He was the sun, an extraordinary beast, and she was—what? Mortal? Something less? Her body was meat, her heartbeat redundant. He strode toward her, the knife out, his placid face screaming want.

"Do you mind," he asked politely, "if I slide my blade under your skin, just a little?"

His smile, it was holy. And when she said, "Yes," his eyes flashed fire.

THE BOY WHO HANGS
THE STARS

Once there was a girl who was sitting by the river. She liked to watch the water, and listen to what it had to say. Usually it was nonsense, but every now and then it came up with something important.

Like today, for instance. "That boy has broken hands!" the river exclaimed, and then it abruptly snapped its mouth shut. The girl noticed that the sun was no longer in her eyes, and she looked up. There stood a strange boy with wild hair and large wings.

"Hello," said the boy.

"Hello," said the girl.

"What are you doing?" asked the boy.

"I'm listening to the water," said the girl.

The boy sat down beside her. "Well, that's interesting. I thought that water didn't really have anything important to say."

"Usually it doesn't."

The girl looked at the strange boy, whose wings fluttered every now and then.

"Your wings, do they ever hurt?"

He shrugged. "Sometimes, when I step on them." He kicked a rock into the river.

The girl and the boy sat in silence for a long time. The water watched them.

"I think that I like you," said the girl after a while.

The boy smiled. "I think that I like you, too."

And that was that.

The next time the girl came down to the river, she was happy to see that the boy was there.

"I brought something for you," she said. From the pocket of her dress, she pulled out a small rock. It was the color of water and it was shiny and it glowed a little. She put it into the boy's hands. It slipped right through them and fell into the river.

She took the boy's hands and held them up to her eyes. Each palm had a round, perfectly circular hole in the middle of it. She could look right through them.

"Oh," she said.

"I told you that he had broken hands!" yipped the river. The winged boy looked very sad.

"I'm sorry that I lost your stone," he said. "It looked very nice."

The girl was too busy thinking about his hands to answer for a while. Finally she said, "How did that happen? Your hands?"

The boy looked at his palms. "I don't know. They've always been this way. I can't hold anything. Watch." He reached down to the water and cupped his hands. When he pulled them back, the water ran right through the holes.

"Broken," the water said again. It tossed the girl's shiny stone back up to her. She held it tightly in her warm hand and thought some more.

That night, she worked hard in her living room, making a present for the boy.

The next day she went back down to the river, and waited and waited for the boy, but he didn't show up. This made the girl very unhappy. But the next time that she went back, the winged boy was sitting on the bank, dangling his bare feet in the water.

"Where were you?" The girl asked him.

"I had to sleep. I have nighttime responsibilities."

"You do? What are they?"

The boy stretched. "Meet me down here in a few nights, and I'll show you. I think you'll like it. What do you have in your hand?"

The girl had almost forgotten the present that she had made. She held it out. The water stone was now dangling on a silver chain.

"Now you won't lose it," she said, and fastened it around the boy's neck. The boy looked happy.

"People don't usually give me things," he said.

"That's probably because you keep dropping them," the girl answered.

"Good point."

The boy put his hand over the new necklace. The girl could see the stone right through the hole in his hand.

"I won't lose this," he promised.

"I know you won't," she said.

"I think I'm hungry," said the girl. "Would you like to come back to my home and get something to eat?"

"Why not?" said the boy, and they stood up and walked through the forest to the village.

The village was full of colors and lights, and flower petals floated through the air. The people rushed back and forth in a hurry, but nobody even took notice of the girl. They all stopped to stare at the boy, however. He tried very hard not to notice.

"This is a pretty village," said the boy.

"It's not so bad," the girl replied.

She walked past old men and young men and women carrying little children, but nobody even turned to look at her. She knelt down to pet a furry dog, which barked and licked her hand, and its owner looked at it strangely. Although not as strangely as he was looking at the boy.

"It's your wings, you know," said the girl. "They're very beautiful. And we've never seen wings on anybody before."

The boy stretched out one wing to examine it, and everybody in the village oohed and aahed. "I've just always had them, so they're perfectly normal to me. How do you fly without your wings?"

The girl smiled at him. "You don't."

This made the boy feel mischievous, so he hopped into the air and flew the rest of the way beside the girl, all the way to her house. He heard people clapping behind him.

"This is a very strange town that you have here," he said.

The girl nodded. "It is." And she opened the door to her home.

There wasn't any furniture inside, just a soft blanket on the floor for a bed. But there were shiny things and hanging things and feathers and tiny castanets that made sounds and chimes and all sorts of flowers that were lying in happy piles here and there.

"I like it this way," said the girl.

They sat down and ate some sort of spiky fruit that was actually quite good when you cut the outside off. Midway through the girl stood up and brushed off her dress.

"I will be right back," she said, and ran out the door. The boy watched her through a window. She ran into a store, picked up a jug of some sort, and left money on the counter. Nobody talked to her. Nobody even looked at her. She came back and poured out two cups of juice. The boy held his cup in his strange hands and frowned.

"Why doesn't anybody talk to you?" he asked her. "They act like they don't even know you're there."

The girl looked up in surprise. "Oh! Well, nobody can see me."

The boy blinked. "Nobody can see you? Nobody at all?"

The girl shook her head. "No. Nobody can hear me, either. Except for the animals. They know that I'm there."

This puzzled the winged boy. "But I can see you."

The girl smiled very big. "I know."

As the boy flew home that night, he thought about the invisible girl who didn't have anybody to talk to except for him. The girl had said something unusual that evening during dinner.

"If your hands were always that way," she'd said, "then it must be for a reason. Why, I don't think that they're broken at all!"

The wind whistled through the holes in his hands as he flew, and maybe for the first time, he didn't really mind.

The next time that the invisible girl walked down to the river, she found a piece of paper wrapped around a rock and tied with a string. "Come back tonight," it said, "and I'll show you."

Show me what? wondered the girl, but she was excited, and put the paper in her pocket.

"What did it say?" asked the river, trying desperately to get a look. But it is common knowledge that rivers can't read.

"He's going to show me," she said.

"Show you what?"

"That's what I thought."

The river played around and wondered what the girl was going to see, and generally made a nuisance of itself, gurgling and whistling loudly. But the girl still sat there, and thought about what the boy might show her. She threw the rock into the river.

"Ow," said the river.

Somehow the girl couldn't manage to make herself be sorry.

It was almost dark. The girl had fallen asleep by the water and woke up to the boy shaking her shoulder. "Are you ready?" he said.

She was.

He said, "Okay, don't let this scare you," and wrapped his arms around her. They flew straight up into the air.

She was indeed scared. Very much. But flying was exciting, too. She tried not to see how there was nothing under her feet.

"Where are we going?" she asked calmly. She was very proud of herself for being so calm.

"We're going to where I sleep. I need to get something. And I told you not to be scared."

"I'm not scared."

The boy laughed. "You're not a very good liar. But you really will be okay. All right. Here is where we want to be."

The boy put her down, very gently. She looked around at where she was.

"You sleep in a nest?"

The boy nodded. He wondered if he should be embarrassed.

"I think it's wonderful!" the girl said, and flopped backward into the nest. The boy smiled and reached for a large, velvet bag.

The bag was very dark and very soft and when the boy shook it, it jingled.

"What's inside?" asked the girl.

"Something very special."

The girl moved closer to get a better look. The boy opened the flap of the bag slowly, and they both peered inside.

"There's light in there!"

"Just watch."

Suddenly a bright little light burst out of the bag and buzzed around their heads. The girl fell back, but the boy merely closed the bag and watched.

The light dove and swirled and sputtered around for a while, and then it landed in the boy's hair with a faint chiming sound. The girl stared at it in wonder.

"It's a star!"

"It is."

The star snuggled down in the boy's hair and made a high, happy sound.

"What is it doing?" she asked.

"It's purring. Stars purr when they're happy, you know. And this is a very happy little star. Hold out your hand."

The girl did as he asked. The star hopped into her hand and chimed brightly. Then it twinkled and purred there, too.

The girl looked at the boy. "You get to play with stars every night?"

The boy shook his head. "Not play, exactly. Work. Here, I'll show you. It's time."

The boy whistled and the star hopped onto his shoulder. He grabbed the girl and the bag and flew into the sky.

The girl was getting a little more used to flying, and wasn't nearly half as nervous as she had been before.

"See? I told you that I was calm," she informed the boy.

"Of course you are."

They flew higher and higher, and finally the boy made his way to a little cloud. "You can sit here," he said, and dropped her on it.

She started to scream, but was surprised when she landed on the cloud like it was a soft pillow. She looked at the boy.

"I thought that clouds couldn't really hold you up. I thought that they were like fog that way."

The boy opened his bag and started poking around inside. The star buzzed around his head. "Those are just stories that people tell. Clouds and fog aren't at all alike, but most people don't know that anymore. But I do." He smiled at the girl. "Are you ready to see what I do every night?"

The girl nodded, and crawled over closer to where the boy was hovering. "Yes, very much." She tried to peek inside of the bag.

The boy brought out a handful of shining stars. They clinked against each other delightfully. "I do this," he said, and threw them into the sky.

The stars flew into the air and stuck in the sky. They twinkled gently. The girl gasped and turned to look at the boy.

"What makes them hang up there like that?"

The boy shrugged his shoulders. "I'm not sure. There aren't hooks. I checked. It is more like they, somehow, stick."

The girl smiled. "I think it's wonderful. Will you please do some more?"

The boy did. He threw out handful after handful of stars, and they all found their place in the sky. Then one of the stars slipped through the hole in his hand, and fell to the ground.

"Oh no," said the boy.

The girl leaned over the edge of the cloud and watched the star fall. "What's wrong?" she asked the boy.

He looked very unhappy. "It's these hands. I told you that I drop things. Now that star is wasted."

"Wasted?" asked the girl in disbelief.

The boy nodded. "Wasted."

The girl smiled. This confused the boy.

"Why are you smiling?" he asked her.

"I don't think that star is wasted at all!" exclaimed the girl.

"What?"

"In my village, whenever we see a star fall like that, it is called a shooting star. A wishing star. They're quite delightful!"

"A...wishing star?"

The girl nodded happily. "Yes! A wishing star. If you make a wish on that star, it will come true. I should know; I've made dozens myself."

"Really?"

"Really!" The girl looked at the boy. "So all of this time, you felt badly about these stars dropping through the holes in your hands. When really, it makes people very happy when they do. Silly boy."

He thought about this. He thought that it made him happy. And when he was happy, his chest hurt. He put his hand over his heart.

"What is it?"

"It's nothing," said the boy. "I think I must be happy. Anyway, I have something else to show you. I think this will help you in the village."

"Really?" asked the girl, excited. But the boy didn't answer. He had already picked her up and was flying back to the nest.

The girl was quite pleased that she didn't scream at all.

When they got back to the nest, the boy dug around until he came up with a small box. "Are you ready?" he asked the girl. She nodded, and he opened it.

Inside were many tiny, tiny little stars. They made small sounds and crawled over each other, seeming very pleased to see the boy and the girl.

"They're beautiful," whispered the girl. "Why are they so small?"

"They're babies," said the boy, and he tried to pick one up. It was so tiny that it slid right through the hole in his hand back into the box. He looked at the girl. "They're too small for me to throw into the sky, so I keep them here until they get bigger. But I think that they get bored."

The girl watched them closely. It looked like the little stars were chasing each other in a circle. "Are they playing?"

"Yes. Stars like to play. But they also like to see things, and they don't get to see much inside of a box. Hold out your hand."

The girl did so. The boy whispered something to the stars, and the girl heard several happy little chimes. She looked at the boy. "What are they doing?"

"Cheering. Just watch."

The little stars swarmed into the girl's hand, and then began to orbit her wrist. They felt cool and bright and made the girl very happy.

"Now you can take them with you," said the boy. "They really are very happy little things, and I think that you'll enjoy them. And they'll get out of the box."

The girl held her wrist up to her face. The stars seemed to be having a lovely time. "Thank you very much!" she said to the boy, and meant it. He smiled.

"You're welcome. But there's another reason that I gave it to you. Come on." He grabbed her and they headed back to the village.

They landed in the center of town, and the girl looked around her. "What is it that I'm supposed to see?"

"I have a theory," the boy said. He waited until he saw an old man walk toward them. Then he politely said, "Hello, sir. Do you see this girl here?"

The girl tugged the boy's sleeve. "I told you that nobody can..."

The old man peered at the girl strangely. "Do I know you?" he asked her.

The girl blinked in surprise. Her mouth fell open. She didn't know what to say. "I...I don't know. Do you?"

The old man studied her face. "There was a girl who looked a lot like you, years ago. But she disappeared after her parents died. And she didn't glow like you do."

"Glow?" asked the girl.

The old man snorted. "She doesn't know that she glows?" he asked the boy. They boy shook his head.

"She was invisible until about half an hour ago, you see."

"Ah," said the old man knowingly. He turned back to the girl. "You," he said matter-of-factly, "glow."

"I do?"

"You do. In fact, there's no color to you, just light. I think that if you didn't glow, I wouldn't see you at all. You're a very lucky young lady."

"Um...thank you, sir," said the girl.

He nodded. "You're welcome." And he slowly walked away.

They watched him leave. Then the boy turned to the girl. "What do you want to do now?"

She was slightly shaken. "I think that I want to go home," she said, and the boy thought that was a fine idea. But it didn't turn out to be as easy as all that.

It really was a very small village, and when the people heard that there was a boy with wings and a glowing girl, they all wanted to see for themselves. Before long there was a crowd of people pressed around the boy and the girl, and it became quite frightening.

"Hey, I know you!" shouted a voice over the crowd. "You look just like your mother!" Soon other people were shouting about how they recognized the girl, or how they wanted to see the boy fly, or wondering how they could get a bracelet of stars for themselves. It took several minutes until the boy and girl managed to push their way into the little house.

"That was terrible," said the girl. Her clothes were torn and her hair had been patted and touched and plucked. One of the stars stuck its tongue out at the people still gathered outside.

"That was rather awkward," agreed the boy as he flopped on the floor. He was missing several long feathers, and his hair was even more wild than usual. "But at least they can see you."

"Yes," said the girl, and she smiled. "I am very happy for that. You don't have to leave, do you?" She looked terrified when the boy started to stand up, and he quickly sat back down. The sky didn't necessarily need stars tonight.

"No, I can stay," he said, and they sat very close together, trying to go to sleep.

But it was impossible. The curious people stayed outside of the house, knocking on the doors and peeking in the windows, and the girl had become quite nervous. The boy thought for a while, and then stood up quickly.

"Let's go," he said, and they ran out of the house and were up in the sky before the people below them had time to realize what was going on.

When they got to the nest, the boy dropped the girl off and flew off to toss a few stars in the sky, just for fun. When he returned, the girl had already fallen asleep. She had her hand stretched out, and as the boy curled up next to her, he thought that her hand looked very empty, somehow. He thought of what he could put in it, but nothing seemed to fit. Finally he slid his own hand inside of hers, and then nodded with satisfaction. That was exactly right. He realized with some delight that his wings tucked just as nicely around two as they did around just himself, and as he drifted off to sleep he put his other hand on his chest, which was hurting him again.

"Why do you keep touching your chest?" the girl asked him a few days later. The river leaned close to listen. It was very curious, as well.

"Because it hurts sometimes," said the boy.

"Do you know why?"

"Not really," he said. He changed the subject. "How are things in the village?"

The girl leaned back in the grass. "Much better, now that people are more used to me. I have some people there that remember my parents. And some of them remember me, too, before I stopped talking. And I guess when you stop talking..."

"People stop seeing you."

"Right." The girl watched the boy out of the corner of her eye. He was rubbing his hand over his heart again.

"You must be hurting more and more lately," she said.

The boy frowned. "I think it is because I have never been so happy. I've never really had a friend before...*ow*."

The girl was worried. "Let me see."

"No."

"But I really want to."

"No," he said again.

"Please?"

The boy sighed, and then slowly unbuttoned his shirt. He pointed to his heart. "See?" he said.

The girl gasped. The boy's heart was beating quite nicely inside of his chest. It wasn't hidden at all.

"Your heart!" she exclaimed.

"What about it?"

"I can see it!"

"Well, of course you can."

The girl shook her head. "No, a heart is usually deep inside of somebody's chest. You can't see mine. Here, take a look." She showed the boy the skin covering her heart.

He was shocked. "But how do you know that it is there?"

"You can feel it. Put your hand here." The girl put the boy's hand on her heart, and she was right. He could feel it beating.

"Amazing," he said.

"Can I look at yours some more?" she asked him.

The difference in their hearts interested him. "Of course."

The girl put her face very close to the boy's heart, and watched it beat. Gently, she stretched out her finger and touched it. It was icy cold.

"It's beautiful," she told the boy. "I like it very much."

This made the boy very happy. His heart started to swell. Immediately, he gasped and clutched at his chest.

"Ah," said the girl. "I see what the problem is."

"What is it?" asked the boy after he caught his breath. He noticed that the girl looked worried.

"Your heart has ice around it," said the girl. She touched his heart again. "That's why it is so cold. Did you know this?"

"Aren't all hearts icy?" he asked.

The girl shook her head. "No, they're not. Ice around a heart is a very bad thing. I remember my mother talking about it before. When you get happy, or love somebody, your heart gets bigger. But if there is ice around it, then there isn't any room for it to grow. It will try, but it will run into the ice and just..."

"Hurt," said the boy. He rubbed his chest.

"Yes."

The boy thought about this. "Sometimes it feels better not to be happy. Because it doesn't hurt as much."

The girl nodded. "Much of the world thinks so. But wouldn't you rather be happy?"

"I don't know," he said simply. "I'm not really sure what happiness is."

The girl bit her lip, studying his heart. She looked up at the boy. "I know how to fix it," she said. She looked worried.

"What's wrong?" asked the boy. "Isn't fixing it a good thing?"

The girl was quiet for a long time. Then she said, "I'm afraid that it is going to hurt you very badly."

The boy was surprised. The girl stood up and pulled a long, sharp branch off of one of the trees. Her face was serious. "Are you ready, boy?"

The boy began to get nervous. He took a step backward.

The girl pointed the branch at the boy and took aim at his heart.

"I don't want you to do this anymore," he told her. "I don't care if I'm never happy. Happiness might be overrated, anyhow."

The girl took a step closer, still holding the branch. The boy put

47

first one hand over his chest, and then the other. The holes in his hands exposed his heart perfectly.

The girl smiled at him, a little sadly, and said, "I love you a little, you know." She rammed the stick right through his hands and into the ice surrounding his heart.

The boy heard a crack and felt something shatter. He screamed and fell in searing pain. He thought that he was going to die.

The girl threw the stick down and ran to the boy.

"Go away!" he screamed. His wings beat the ground in spasms. "Go away go away GO AWAY!"

The girl stood there for a second, unsure of what to do, but when she saw the hateful way that the boy looked at her, she turned and ran through the forest.

Several days went by and there was no sign of the boy. Night after night the girl looked anxiously out of her window into the sky, but there were never any stars. The nights were very dark and cold. The people in the village began to comment on it.

"I think that I killed the boy who hangs the stars," the girl said to the old woman sitting next to her. They had grown quite fond of each other over the last few days.

"Nonsense," said the old woman. "I'm sure that he's just resting. Or maybe he went to visit the sea."

The girl didn't believe this for a minute. The old woman realized it immediately.

"Perhaps he's just brooding then, dear. Young boys do so love to brood."

"I don't know," said the girl. "I think I may have killed him."

"I doubt it, dear. It is very hard to kill a person."

The girl looked at the old woman. "I stabbed him in the heart with a sharp stick."

The old woman opened her mouth, and then shut it again. Finally, she spoke. "Who really needs the stars anyway? They aren't very useful when you think about it." Then she got to her feet and shuffled off.

That night the girl walked down to the river. Even the stars around her wrist seemed lonely. She sat by the water, who, for the first time, had absolutely nothing to say.

"Say something. Anything!" pleaded the girl.

The water tried very hard to help the girl.

"Nutmeg," it said. "Squeakriot. Gimberschnickel."

"Thank you," said the girl, and she was grateful.

The water didn't say anything again for a long time, and then it suddenly piped up. "You're crying!" it yelled.

"What?" said the startled girl.

"You're crying for the broken-handed boy!" The water sounded triumphant.

"No, I'm not!" The girl was indignant.

"Then what is this, then?" The river popped something round and smooth out of the water toward the girl. She caught it and held it in her hands. It was a large, white pearl.

"It's a pearl," she said.

The water waited expectantly.

"You giving me a pearl doesn't mean that I'm crying!" The girl was getting angry. Suddenly she noticed that a tear slid down her cheek, fell into the water, and turned into a pearl. In fact, there was quite a large pile of pearls beneath her in the river.

"Oh," she said softly.

The water snickered.

The baby stars around her wrist seemed absolutely delighted at the pearl, and swarmed around it. They pulled it out of her hand and started to chase each other around her wrist, bouncing the tear-pearl back and forth between them like a ball. It was the cheeriest that they had been in days.

"Find him," said the water, and it began to hum.

The girl wanted very much to find him, but she didn't know how. They had always flown to the nest, and she didn't know how to get there from the ground.

"I wish to find him," she said. "Very much."

Suddenly she saw a bright light, and heard a familiar sound. She turned around to see a cascade of stars falling from a tall tree not too far away. The stars clinked and glittered and chimed as they landed on the ground and in the water.

"Wishing stars!" she said, and ran as fast as she could toward the light. There were more stars than she had ever seen, and on each one she made her wish. "I wish to find the boy! I wish to find the boy!"

When she finally reached the tree, she blinked the stars out of her eyes and looked way, way up. She thought she saw a nest at the top of the tree. Taking a deep breath, she started to climb.

The tree was higher than she had originally thought, and difficult to climb. The branches tore her dress and skin, but she kept climbing. The stars continued to fall, much more slowly, and they got caught in her hair, and eyelashes, but she didn't stop to shake them out. She was concentrating too hard on making her way to the very top of the tree. Finally she reached the nest, and using the last of her strength, she pulled herself inside.

She lay gasping for a minute, and then looked around. There lay the boy.

"Hi," he said. He looked too weak to move. "I'm glad that you came."

"Hi," said the girl. She was too weak to move, too, and smiled at the boy. "I'm glad that I didn't kill you earlier."

"It kind of felt like you did," said the boy. He didn't sound at all mad.

"I'm very sorry," said the girl, quite honestly. "I thought that I was doing the right thing, and maybe I wasn't." She took a deep breath and managed to crawl a little closer to the boy. She lay down again, and looked at him. "Are you all right?"

"I think so," he said. "I'm feeling much better today. It was quite bad for a while, and I was so angry that the ice started to come back. I got rid of it myself, though, you see."

The girl was surprised. "Yourself? But with what?" The girl didn't see any sharp sticks around. The boy looked sad.

"I used this," he said, and put his hand weakly up to the necklace that she had made him. The stone was shattered in half. "It broke," he said needlessly.

"That doesn't matter at all!" said the girl. "How is your heart? May I see?"

The boy nodded and the girl moved his shirt and peered at his heart. It was beating a little weaker than usual, and it seemed larger. The ice was nowhere to be seen. The girl touched it with her finger, and it was very warm. She smiled.

"I think that maybe you don't have to worry about the ice coming back," she said. The boy looked pleased for a bit. He didn't seem to notice when the stars hopped off of the girl's wrist and swarmed around his neck.

"So did you see the wishing stars?" he asked.

"Yes!" said the girl. "I was hoping to find you, and I was pleased when I saw them! I wouldn't have found you otherwise, you know."

"Yes, I thought that you would see them. What are they doing?

Hey, wait a minute!" The boy noticed that the little stars had taken the shattered stone out of the necklace and had tossed it out of the nest. The boy tried to grab it, but it slipped through the hole in his hand. One of the stars said something to him quite firmly, and the boy quieted.

"What did it say?" asked the girl.

"It chastised me, and told me to let them finish. Stars, even baby ones, can be quite firm, you know."

The stars continued to swarm around his neck, and when they had finished, the boy had something new and whole hanging from the silver chain. It was a large white pearl.

"Where did this come from?" he asked.

"Well, um..."

The girl didn't really want to say, but the stars hopped all over each other to tell the story. The girl was very embarrassed, and looked at her hands.

"I think," said the boy, "that this makes me very happy." They both looked down at his heart, which was swelling bigger and bigger. The boy put his hand over it. So did the girl.

It was a beautiful feeling. It didn't hurt at all.

UNTIED

The crazy man outside of my office window had been threatening to jump for at least two and a half hours. His ex-wife had remarried, he said. She had moved on. Her new husband was a doctor. Said doctor had written a novel. He worked closely with Operation Smile, Habitats for Humanity, and picketed for women's rights. He knitted sweaters for cold, underprivileged children.

"How could he do all that if he's a *doctor*?" I shouted, kneeling on my desk so I could hang my head out of the window. The crazy man paused. He thought. He allowed that maybe his wife—*ex*-wife—had allowed a few half-truths to surface, in order to make the new doctor-husband seem extra stellar. This seemed to perk the crazy man up some. "Maybe he's just a really lousy doctor," I said, and the crazy man smiled big.

"I like you!" he declared, and then he whistled cheerily for the next half hour. A little disappointed, I sat back at my desk to work.

It was impossible. The crazy man was distracting. He wore a horrible, flesh colored tie that did absolutely nothing for his blond hair and rosy coloring. It snapped in the wind like a pirate's flag. It pranced around his neck, pressing its face against my window and *nya-nya-nyaed* at me like an ill-mannered school boy. I couldn't take my eyes off of it. It noticed this, and began to undulate around, running its tongue over its lips and wagging its eyebrows suggestively.

I climbed back up on my desk, knocking my folder to the ground in my haste.

"Your tie," I yelled.

"What?" He jumped about a foot; not a good thing to do out on a window ledge fourteen stories over Manhattan.

"Your *tie*," I practically screamed. The tie looked at me in confusion. So did the man.

"My tie?" he shrieked back.

"Yes, your tie!" Silence. "I hate it!"

The man looked hurt. "You hate my tie?"

"Yes!" My throat was starting to hurt. "It's...it's..." The tie glared at me. "It's obscene. It's the wrong color. It's lewd and suggestive... and I think it's trying to pick me up."

The man looked shocked. The tie looked bored. I looked stupid.

"Well, okay, I'm going back in," I said, and did just that.

The man was silent for a long time. The tie was obviously enraged. It beat against the window, snarling. It made threatening gestures. It danced provocatively around and then shook its finger as if to say, "No no, you can't touch." I threw my hands up in exasperation.

The man, his back still toward me, knocked tentatively on my window. I sighed, climbed back up on my desk, and leaned outside. "Yes?"

He said something quietly that I couldn't hear.

"Come again?"

"I said, my wife gave it to me."

"What?"

"The tie. The tie! I said that my wife—*ex*-wife—gave me the blasted tie! I knew it was horrible. It was much too bland. But she gave it to me, so I wore it, and now here I am, ready to greet the pavement, and I'm still wearing this...tie..." Thankfully, a good part of what he said was lost in the wind. The tie, however, looked appalled.

"So ditch the tie," I said. My attention was on my leg, which was cramping up.

He turned his face away and closed his eyes haughtily. "You're not taking this seriously,"

I rubbed my knotted calf furiously.

"Look," I said. "I work a horrible, soul-crushing job with a lascivious rat for a boss and a glory hound coworker who steals all of my credit. My chair is broken, the "Y" on my keyboard sticks, and all I have to look forward to is some lousy steamed vegetables and a crossword for lunch. I'm sorry that your ex-wife moved on. I'm sorry you're so distraught over it. I'm especially sorry that you're so good-looking, single, and obviously so deranged. I have a very busy schedule, and you and your harlot of a tie have put me far behind. Now either jump or crawl back inside because I don't have the time to be kneeling here hanging out of my office window like this."

He was silent, but only for a minute. "What's your name?"

"Absinthe."

"It fits."

"Shut up and jump."

"Now that's not very nice."

I gritted my teeth and crawled back into my office, vowing not to speak again until I was identifying his body to the policemen downstairs. I slid off of my desk and hopped around on my leg to ease the cramping, cursing colorfully in my head while I did so.

The blond man was watching me. I looked resolutely away and pretended not to care. His tie was equally enamored with my performance. I hopped around a few more times and then sank gracefully into my chair as though nothing had happened.

All of the hopping and crawling and hanging out of the window had forced my hair from its careful, neat-yet-not-prim updo into a crazy mass of curls that hung in my face. I blew them out of my eyes and began typing. Ignoring the crazy man, of course—

Who had turned around completely so that he was facing the window with his palms pressed against the glass. Not that I was looking. Because I wasn't.

I stared hard at my reports. Something about the Traevoli case wasn't fitting together, and I gnawed nervously on my pen as I tried to figure it out. Oh! I think I know where I saw this before. I dragged my heavy briefcase onto my lap and snapped it open. Digging around, I finally pulled out a paper with a ring of coffee and a lipstick smudge on the top. Hey, when you gotta blot, you gotta blot, okay? One day I'll keep wonderful, immaculate files. I just know it.

Holding the paper up to the screen, I squinted at it for a while until I came to the source of the problem. Ugh, that's it. I must have mistyped it while concentrating on the crazy ma—I mean, while being distracted by nothing at all.

It took seconds to delete the wrong information and retype the correct names and numbers. There. I leaned back in my chair and sighed happily. I have saved the firm from certain disaster! Imminent destruction! They shall all laud me and shower me with gifts and a toe-curling raise. Or at least a decent paycheck. I shook my hands over my head like a champion.

"Good heavens, you're absolutely insane."

I stiffened in my chair, and whipped my head up. My hair obscured my vision for a second, but I tossed it out of my eyes with a practiced jerk of the head.

"You!" I pointed at the crazy man, who had inched closer and was now standing in my window. "Haven't you jumped yet?"

He shook his head, not at all hurt. "Not yet."

"Are ya gonna?"

"Now that doesn't seem like a very neighborly thing to say to somebody. Didn't your mama raise you better?"

I kicked my shoes off, put my feet on the desk and crossed my ankles. "My mama would have pushed you off herself by now. You are incredibly frustrating. In or out."

"What's that?"

"In or out. You can't hover in my window all day like a maniac. It's poor form."

I could see him thinking about it. In fact, I could practically hear the wheels turning in his head. He eyed my stark, gray office, and then glanced almost longingly over his shoulder at the ledge.

I felt my eyes narrowing. "Hey, you. I see the way you're looking at the place. You really think jumping would be preferable?"

He shrugged and leaned in a little farther. "Well, it is pretty dreary. I mean, maybe if it were more welcoming, or something. Out here, I can see the people and the birds. There's a lot to look at. But your office..." He trailed off mercifully. Then he added, "You need some art."

I felt crestfallen. "I don't have any art."

"That's apparent."

"I don't even know how to go look for art."

He was taken back. "Really? It's not hard. You just wander

around and find something that speaks to you." He was looking at me in a new light.

I pulled my formally jaunty feet off of my desk and tucked them under my chair. "I am an art loser."

"No, you're not."

"Yes, I am. There is not an artsy bone in my body. I know nothing about color and light and movement and shape. I'd pick out a poster and somebody with taste would shame me into putting it back. It's just too daunting." My stomach growled. "And now I'm hungry."

He almost smiled. "For your steamed vegetables and the daily crossword?"

I groaned and dropped my head on the desk. "Move over, fella. I'm jumping with you."

I heard him moving around, felt the desk shift under his weight. I looked up. "What are you doing?"

"Coming in. We're going to go get you some lunch."

"But your glorious plans to end your life. I'd hate to mess them up!"

He shook his head and hopped off of the desk onto the floor. "I'll get over it," he said. He held out a hand. "Ready?"

I reached out to take it, but drew my hand back again. His tie was watching me with wide eyes. It was drooling a little bit.

He followed my gaze, and then pulled the beige tie from his neck. He held it outside of the window. The tie gasped and then started to scream out some very crude language. I ran to the window to watch.

Beautiful Crazy Man winked at me and let the tie go. The tie whooped and hollered and shrieked as it drifted almost to the ground before being hit by a speeding taxi. I smiled. Served it right.

"So," he said casually, looking not at all guilty about his nasty tie murder. "Lunch?"

"Lunch," I said.
"And we shop for art?"
"Don't push it."
He reached out and took my hand.
Well, maybe a little art.

THE CONTAINER OF SORROWS

There was a girl. She sat at a white desk in a white room with her hands folded neatly in her lap.

Peter stood before her with his pockets turned out.

"I don't have anything to give you," he said. He spoke very quietly. Shame does that.

She didn't move, but he thought that she shook her head.

"I don't need anything like that," she told him. "I do not desire your buttons or baubles, although I am sure that they are quite lovely."

He thought that she smiled, but she did not actually do that, either.

"I don't understand," he confessed. He shifted from foot to foot. She really did smile then, but only in her eyes. He bit his lip and continued. "I thought...that you wanted something from me. In exchange for your help."

"Oh, but I do." Her skin was white, and her hair even whiter, but only just. When she smiled—if she smiled—her lips were disconcertingly red. The rest of the time they were only the palest of pink. He had the impression that something parasitic sucked the breath from those lips while she slept, but what could he do about it?

"Please tell me what you desire."

"I want to be happy."

"Then I will help you."

She pulled a ceramic jar out of nowhere. It was the color of sky and looked cool to the touch. He flexed his fingers.

"This is the Container of Sorrows, Peter. Do you understand?"

"Yes." He didn't.

Her lips barely twitched but it was as if the snow melted and he tasted spring.

"This is how you will be happy. Tell me one of your sorrows. I will keep it here for you, and the burden from that particular sorrow will be no more."

He felt stupid and stared at his shoes. They had holes in the toes.

"Do you...not wish happiness?"

Her voice was strangely brittle, as if she were trying not to cry. He was hurting her somehow, he decided, but that didn't make any sense. He took a deep breath.

"I miss my mother," he said, and the words fell from his mouth like vapor. The girl opened the jar, and the mist zipped inside. She closed the lid with a satisfying click.

"There," she said, and her smile was real this time, genuine. "Don't you feel better?"

He thought about his mother. Her warm brown hair, the apron that she used when she baked cupcakes. He thought about her more aggressively. The police telling his father that they had discovered a broken body. The funeral in a town without rain.

"I don't feel sad," he said in wonder, and the girl looked pleased. She kissed him, and he woke up.

Peter's lips burned where she had touched him, and he kept his fingers pressed there for most of the day. When the boys razzed him about his poorly trimmed hair, he didn't mind so much. When they taunted him about his mother being a whore who got what was coming to her, he was surprised to find that he didn't care at all. He ate dinner silently and changed into his worn pajamas without being asked. He brushed his teeth and climbed into bed with an eagerness that would have been pitifully endearing if anyone had seen it.

Sleep came instantly, and there she was. She was wearing white flowers in her hair.

"Did you have those flowers yesterday?" he asked her.

Her cheeks flushed delicately. "No."

Peter didn't know what to say. "I had a better day at school than usual. Thank you."

The girl again brought the smooth blue container out of thin air. "Tell me another sorrow, Peter. Tomorrow will be even better."

He thought. "I'm tired of being called poor."

The mist of words spiraled into the Container of Sorrows. He nodded his head once, and she nodded back in a very serious manner.

And thus it went. His sorrows disappeared. "I hate seeing dead birds. I wish that I had a friend. My father doesn't notice me."

The jar devoured his sorrows with an agreeable hunger. The pale girl's lips turned up all of the time and her eyes began to sparkle. Peter grew more confident at school. He stood up straight. He looked people in the eye. He made friends.

He was almost happy.

On the last night that he went to her, something in the air had shifted. The atmosphere was holding its breath, and it was undeniable.

"Hey," Peter said, leaning casually on the white desk. "There's only one sorrow that I have left."

"Only one?" asked the girl with something that sounded exquisitely close to hope. Her eyes shone. Her white hair and red lips were glossed with fragile expectation. She produced the Container of Sorrows and carefully removed its lid. Peter's sorrows ghosted around inside, smelling of lavender and brokenness.

"Natalia Bench never looks at me at school."

The vaporous sorrow swirled from his lips and settled into the jar. The girl's white fingers didn't move, so Peter put the lid back on for her.

He smiled. "Now I'll be brave enough to talk to her tomorrow. Thank you very much, Girl of Sorrows. I am happy."

The girl held the jar very close, and she looked up at Peter. Her lips were pale, strawberries buried under layers of ice. He was reminded of that feeling that he had once, long ago, where he thought that something supped from her lips at night. How frightened she must be. How alone.

How silly.

"Goodbye," he said, and kissed her cheek. Had her touch once burned? She was ice under his skin. She was a corpse. Peter turned and walked away without looking back.

There was a girl. She sat at a white desk in a white room where she wept, clutching a container full of somebody else's sorrows.

DEADENED

The garden gnome didn't start talking to her until Todd died. She didn't know if this was because it never had anything particularly interesting to say before, or if it felt nervier with Todd out of the picture, or because she had simply gone crazy with rage and grief. Either way, facts were facts, and Boris the Lawn Gnome hadn't said a word until Todd had been moldering for a while.

In fact, Todd's decay was what prompted the conversation in the first place.

Antonella was digging around in the tiny patch of dirt that constituted the garden of her condo. She wasn't planting anything, necessarily. She didn't know how. She just pulled things that grew, hoping some of them were weeds, knowing some must have been flowers, and the fashionably ironic kitschy lawn gnome glowered at her.

"I wonder what Todd looks like, don't you, Antonella?"

His voice was deep and dark and full of gnomish things, but he rolled his r's perfectly. She was vaguely impressed.

"You use a lovely Spanish accent," she told the gnome.

"Thank you. I bet Todd is decomposing nicely."

Antonella stuck her hands in the dirt, moved her fingers around like roots searching for water, like worms in Todd's skin.

"You think about it, too, eh, Boris?"

The gnome didn't really shrug, which made sense because he was made of ceramic or resin or clay, but she knew that he would if he could.

"I think about a lot of things. Mostly what you think about."

She sat back on her heels, rubbed the sweat from her eyes with the back of a filthy hand.

"Because I'm crazy? Because I'm projecting my grief on an intimate object?"

"Inanimate."

"Excuse me?"

"Inanimate. Intimate is a different thing."

She smiled, nearly. One side of her mouth hitched and almost held, but then she remembered that she was alone, and Todd was dead, and she was talking to a cheap piece of kitsch that she had never really liked anyway.

"Stop correcting me, figment-of-my-imagination."

"Stop using words that you've only read and never heard. You're pronouncing them incorrectly."

"Todd used to say the same thing."

The garden gnome looked sage. Or wise. Perhaps crafty. It let Antonella's words hang in the air, Heavy With Meaning.

"Enough, funny little creature. I know you aren't him. He wouldn't come back and haunt an…an *inanimate* object like this."

"Great pronunciation."

"Thank you. Now I need to go."

She stood up, dusting her hands off on her bare legs. She

wondered if she should pat the gnome on the head or if that would be insulting. Instead, she politely nodded, and thought perhaps he politely nodded back. If the resin would let him.

"I'll be here," he said. His gnomish accent was so thick and deep that she strained to understand, then she shook her head.

"No, you won't. I'll take a nap and everything will set itself to rights. Goodbye, little friend."

She stepped inside and shut the door behind her. The sound filled her with a strange sort of sadness.

That night she dreamed that she was a rabbit, a black one, and she hopped to and fro, doing adorable rabbity things. Then she took a knife from the kitchen and lopped off her own ears.

She woke alone in her room, tearless, but raised her fingers to touch her earlobes. They were soft and had tiny chips of pink diamonds in them, and most importantly, they weren't lopped at all, but intact.

Todd's earlobes probably weren't intact. They were likely in pieces, or had turned into mush, or whatever happened when the body of a loved one was shoved under the ground. "Put to rest with care," people said. "Entombed with love." As if they were a treasure, a priceless thing that needed to be fed back to the earth, buried, and marked with a cemetery's map.

Antonella knew that wasn't the case. People stuck things in the ground to hide. Shut them in a box and heaved them into the ocean of dirt so they would be forgotten.

"Well, I can't forget," she said aloud, and sat up in bed. The strap of her nightgown slipped down one brown shoulder and she tugged it absently back into place.

She dressed for work and ran through her boring job, answering phones and scheduling appointments, and then she came home with a bag of take-out from Ying's. Ying's chicken was nubby and the sauces were sometimes hit or miss, but it was cheap and the woman who took orders always smiled at Antonella with her eyes as well as her mouth, and that was reason enough to go.

"Boris," she greeted, as she did every day when she came home and passed him on the step. His bushy brows didn't move, and he regarded his tiny lawn with the air of royalty, red lips clamped firmly on the end of his pipe.

Antonella unlocked the door and set the food on the clean table. She hesitated, looking at Todd's empty chair, and then sighed. She headed outside.

"Come on, you," she said, and picked up Boris the Gnome. She shook the dirt from his yellow, pointed shoes and brought him in.

"Better insane than lonely," she explained, and set him on Todd's chair. She settled into the other and dug into the food, using cheap wooden chopsticks to eat directly from the carton.

"I understand," Boris said, and his rough voice was kind.

"Sure, you do. Here's to us."

Antonella lifted her fountain drink in salute, and then took a sip through the straw.

"This is only the beginning," Boris assured her.

"The beginning of what?"

That thick, mushroom of an accent. It obscured what he said. She thought she heard him say "the end".

Boris the UnTodd had been living in the house for a while. Mainly in the kitchen, where he perched on the counter and surveyed his domain in the sunshine. Then he gradually moved to the living room, where he developed a particular penchant for bad Kung Fu movies and Judge Judy.

"Mind leaving the TV on when you go to work today?" he asked. "Judge Judy is dealing with two especially vile deadbeats. The woman cut the whiskers off her boyfriend's cat. Judy's sense of justice…"

"You need to pitch in with the electricity bill," she said, but did as he asked. She discovered that she was doing that a lot. He'd suggest something and she'd obey. "Try something different with your hair," or "Why don't we lighten this place up a bit with some yellow paint?" or "The drug dealer down the street deserves to have his car set on fire."

This last one shocked her a bit.

"Excuse me?" she said, and Boris managed to tear his eyes away from Judge Judy's long, black robes long enough to flick a glance in Antonella's direction.

"He deserves it. He sells drugs to school children. How despicable is *that*?"

"Very. But setting The Candy Man's car on fire? Isn't that a little…"

"Gutsy? Apt. Justified."

"Crazy."

He snorted and his eyes rolled back to his Judy. She was radiant in her righteous anger, her hair standing around her sharp nose like a halo of darkness.

"You worry too much about such things, Antonella."

"But that's…that's arson! That's pyromania."

"Think of it more as retribution. Or prevention if that's more appetizing."

She didn't want to admit it, but the idea of it was delicious. Sneaking over. Dousing the upholstery with gasoline. Using a match or a lighter or a crème brulee torch or

"That's the ticket, sweetheart. But something you can do from a distance. You don't want to get burned."

"You know, Boris, the more that I think about it, it does sound like a good idea."

"Let me know how it goes."

Antonella felt something coursing through her body. Something new and different.

Excitement.

"It's been a long time since I was excited," she whispered to Boris later that night. Her black hair was pulled up and stuffed under a dark hat. She wore one of Todd's old Metroid t-shirts and fairly danced from foot to foot.

"Go," he commanded in his dark voice. "Be careful. When you come back, tell me all about it."

She wished she could take him. Wished for it so hard and with such force that it nearly felled her, nearly drove her to her knees, but then again, maybe it was simply nerves. Or seeing Todd's old clothes, which she had kept hidden away in her closet. But a woman, especially a woman committing a crime, couldn't be running around with a heavy garden gnome in her backpack. Why, it just isn't done. It's ridiculous.

She left, then, creeping down the road on her small, quiet feet. Sweet Antonella, a faceless woman on the street. Going anywhere, about her evening, nothing suspicious or untoward here, thank you very much. She slid past overflowing garbage cans and skipped over puddles of murky, oil-stained water. To the Candy Man's house and, more importantly, his car.

"He's a bad person," she told herself as she pulled a small water bottle out of her backpack. She opened the lid, and the intense smell of gasoline made her eyes water. "Bad people deserve bad things. In fact, doing bad things to bad people is a *good* thing, right? Perhaps I'm actually a hero."

When she saw the man driving down the street with his old El Camino, parking on street corners and hanging around elementary schools, he never had his window rolled up. She had hoped that perhaps it was broken, or the Candy Man was so full of hubris that he felt safe, untouchable, and kept the window open to prove it. And she was in luck because the window was down and the worn, doggy-smelling upholstery was exposed and vulnerable.

She crouched by the car, hidden from the house, and emptied the water bottle of gasoline all over the seat. She threw it inside of the car, lit a match, closed her eyes, and murmured something surprisingly close to a prayer.

"Burn, you son of a—"

The rest of the words were caught in the small blaze that erupted when the match touched bare front seat stuffing. It caught fast-food wrappers and moved across the filthy seat with a speed that took Antonella back.

"Run," she told herself, and then she did.

Running, stumbling, nearly falling, she fled along the back fences, her blood and mind racing. She flew into her house, slamming the door behind her. Antonella leaned against her, breathing hard.

"How was it?" Boris the Gnome asked. His voice was thick and warm.

Antonella's smile cut all the way to the corners of her face.

71

"Oh, it was good," she said, and picked the gnome up. She swung him around, dancing through the apartment. "Better than good. It was positively..."

"Devilish?" he asked, and she laughed and kissed his cold, resin beard.

"Devilish," she agreed, and that night she watched the fire on the news, and hugged Boris the Devilish Gnome to her, and when she slept, she set him on the nightstand next to her.

"Keep watch?" she asked, and immediately felt silly. Asking a lawn gnome to do anything was just too bizarre to believe. But as she turned on her side and fell asleep, dreams of fires and lopped bunnies and dead Todds ready to haunt her, she felt a hand brush against her hair. It was warm and soft and very, very real.

"Boris, hand me that wrench," Antonella commanded, and held out her hand. The wrench slid obediently into her palm.

"What are we doing tonight, my girl?"

Gone was the thick accent, the sound of dust and ancient mountains. Boris sounded younger, spryer, and the gravel of his voice had been sanded, his vocal gears grinding more smoothly.

Antonella tightened things and loosened things and prayed she was doing it right. After all, Todd had done all the upkeep pretty much ever since they had been kids. Now she was a woman with a wrench, and she was proud and wary all at once.

She hefted it. A nice weight. She took a practice swing, and Boris' cherry red lips parted in a smile.

"Yes," he said simply, and that was that.

As to who, there would be no question. The neighbors next

door had been getting into it every night. Or more to the point, he had been getting drunk and loud and angry. *She* had been getting punches to the face, it sounded like. Tonight, those tables were going to turn.

"And then maybe a movie, Todd?" She caught herself, flushed. "I'm sorry. Boris. Of course, I meant to say Boris."

He patted her hand.

"It's all right, my dear. After all, your Todd is dead and buried and probably bones and slime right now. I wonder? Maybe we should look the decomposition rate after the movie."

Antonella's brows furrowed, but the shine of the wrench caught her eye, and the future seemed somehow bright again.

This time when the neighbors began to scream, Antonella grit her teeth, rolled up her sleeves, and joined in the screaming. By the time the police came, the man was lying dead on the floor, tufts of hair and pieces of skull missing. The woman babbled about some stranger that came in swinging something heavy and gleaming and looking like some sort of demon from Hell or an angel from God, she couldn't quite tell. And Antonella was sitting in a movie theatre, sharing a bag of popcorn with Boris, who emerged from her backpack and was sitting on the seat beside her.

"This seat would have been empty, if not for you," she said. She wrapped her arm around him during the scary parts and patted his hat happily during the funny parts and thought about Todd and how his jaw would most likely fall off his face if he laughed at anything right now.

"Now's not the time to think about it," Boris said gruffly, and somebody in the theatre shushed him. He said something back, something dark and filthy and ancient sounding, and nobody shushed him again.

And life was good for a while. Antonella discovered that she had not only a penchant for fires, but a talent as well. She moved up from cars to strip bars and night clubs, then eventually the homes of corrupt policemen and senators. With each arson and assault and attempted murder she became stronger and more clever.

Boris changed, too. He often argued with her now. Told her to leave victims she wanted to take. Told her to leave havoc she wanted to make.

"Leave me alone, Todd," she said angrily one night. She had cut her hair and lined her eyes with deep black. Todd's name had been tattooed on her chest, right above her heart. Upside down, so she could look down and read it. "You're becoming a pest."

"Where did this come from?" Boris answered back. He puffed angrily on his pipe, stalking through the condo with his pointy boots. "This thirst for blood."

"I'm doing good things."

"It won't absolve you."

She glared at him, and he glared back.

"I don't need absolved."

"Sure, you do."

"What do you know? You're a stupid garden gnome."

"And you're a killer."

She gasped, then bared her teeth.

"I only kill those who deserve to be killed."

"Aren't we suddenly righteous?"

"What are you implying, Boris?"

He shrugged. "I'm not implying anything."

She felt the expression change on her face, and it felt ugly. Frightening.

"You'd better shut your mouth, Todd."

74

Boris looked at her with Todd's gray eyes. Todd's slow blink. When he opened his mouth, he had Todd's voice and his careful way of speaking.

"Todd's dead, Antonella. You know that. Better than anyone, you know that. Right? Don't you remember?"

She took a step back. Boris was wearing Todd's clothes. Todd's face.

"This can't be," she whispered, and pressed herself against the wall.

Boris the Todd shrugged. With each step he grew taller, stood straighter, until they were face to face.

"Why can't it be?" He asked. The skin on his forehead parted, a gory red sea, and the ocean of blood overflowed its banks, ran into his dark hair and eyes.

"No, please, Todd. I can't see this again. I can't."

He stopped, nose to nose with her, his Antonella, his best friend, his platonic love, his killer.

"Can't see what? What can't you see?"

Specks of skull and brain matter ran with the blood. A clump of hair clung to the frame of his glasses.

"Antonella, you're worrying me. Are you all right?" His eyes were full of concern, compassion, before the eye socket around one smashed in on itself with the sound of…almost pennies in a jar, but duller. Cockroaches in a sock. The sound of things that shouldn't ever be heard, by anyone.

Antonella squeezed her eyes shut, covered her ears, and screamed. She screamed until she ran out of breath, then she breathed in (Todd's blood, the breath from his dead lungs, the air that touched the diseased and decaying Todd) and screamed again.

"Stop it! Look at me!" He begged, but she could hear by the

sound of his voice that his vocal cords were rotting out, that he was crumbling to dust in front of her, and she couldn't bear to see.

"I'm sorry, Todd! I didn't mean to. It was an accident at first. It was."

She was crying, now, remembering the taste of his gray matter, the way that he had tripped over some roots in the California Redwoods, hitting his head on a rock, and the sound of it. He was mostly alive, or maybe mostly dead.

"Somebody that close to death? I did you a favor. It was a *favor,*" she insisted, and her ears filled with the sound of skull and body and their childhood bond breaking as she clubbed him at first with a big stick, but then went for a rock instead, because it was harder, and stronger, and would kill him quicker, and he'd stop making those *sounds*, which at first were her name, and then the word "why", and then eventually they didn't make sense anymore.

"You wouldn't die! Why wouldn't you die? You just kept hurting and hurting and all that pain would be gone if you'd just die, Todd!"

"And you'd be free."

It wasn't Todd's voice anymore. It was thickly accented and reminded her of worms digging holes, of dirt being deposited in different places so the flowers could grow.

"Boris?"

He puffed on his pipe. Or at least she thought he did, but she couldn't be sure. He didn't move. He was cast of resin. Poorly painted. Cheaply bought and meant to stand guard over an empire of geraniums and strawberry plants. Not meant to become a familiar to a burgeoning witch. Not meant to be a psychotherapist to a crazy girl.

Just kitsch. That's all he was.

Boris waggled his brows. When he spoke, his voice sounded like Antonella's.

"But he was so kind. So gracious to look after you, wasn't he? After all your episodes. Without Todd, you'd be living in a home for the disturbed somewhere. But he vouched for you. Said he'd take care of you. And he did a good job, didn't he? Gave up so much for the little girl he knew from home."

"Stop it, Boris."

"Gave up a chance at his own life."

"I said stop it!"

"Who would marry a guy who had a crazy ward? No wife. No little Toddlets."

"Enough!"

"You're ungrateful. You never thanked him, not once. Do you realize that?"

A scream. Primal. Gutteral. Coming from her or Boris the UnTodd or Boris the Todded, she couldn't tell. But there was screaming and a shattering sound as she threw the gnome to the floor. Picked him up and threw him again. Took the wrench from the counter and beat the pieces into smaller pieces, into the smallest pieces, until she couldn't hear the sound anymore.

She wept.

She took a shower.

She slept.

She dreamed.

In the morning, she was surprised to discover resin shards all over her kitchen floor. Did a cat get in during the night? Knock over a flowerpot? She cleaned it up. She went to work, answered phone calls, scheduled appointments, picked up a cheap hamburger and a soda at a drive-through, and came home.

It was lonely without her Todd. He'd been gone so long. She

wondered what he looked like now, in his casket. If he was reduced to bones, or if it was still too early.

"Oh, I'm sure he's bones by now," her Cookie Monster cookie jar said in his cheery, growly voice. "Bones and maybe pieces of sinew. We should check, Antonella. Would you like to go to the graveyard? Just say hi? See him? Right now?"

A PLACE OF BEAUTY

She left her husband because of him.

There was no scandal. There was no affair. One day she was struggling off of the subway, and she saw a man in a long coat, staring at the skyscrapers like a tourist. Only she'd seen him before at this same stop, and she realized that he lived here. He lived in the city, yet he still devoured the buildings and sidewalks and yes, even the graffiti as though he were starving. He loved this city, loved it insanely. He, as Edgar Allan Poe had so yearningly put it, "loved with a love that was more than love," and this made her realize something: her husband did not love her. Oh, he had grown quite used to her, which isn't the same thing, not at all. He'd most likely be upset when she left, and might miss the warm spots that her body created in the house where she slept and bathed. He might perk his ears listening for the sounds of her walking the floor at night, as she did quite often when she couldn't sleep, but these things are so very different from love. His having grown comfortable with her presence wasn't enough for her anymore.

"Oh, Gary," she said that evening, after turning down the

television. He promptly turned it back up, so she flipped the TV off. He turned it back on, so she flipped it off, unplugged it, and then pushed the entire thing to the floor with a mighty and quite delicious crash.

"Oh, Gary," she said again, a shining goddess amidst the glass and wires of the shattered television, "this isn't going to work, you see. I have grown very tired of you, and I don't think that I love you anymore. And you, well, you never loved me in the first place, so why don't we part amicably? Do stop fussing; I'll purchase you a new television."

Gary made sounds like he wanted her to stay, but after she crossed her arms over her chest and said, "Really? You do? Why?" he couldn't think of a compelling reason.

"I like that you make food. I like having somebody to share my bed whenever I want. I like coming home to a clean house and I like the way that my laundry smells," he said rather lamely.

She smiled then, and kissed him on his cheek, and said that almost all of these things could be accomplished with a good maid, and that all of them could be accomplished with a bad one. She wrote down the name of their fabric softener, put on her best hat, and picked up her suitcase.

"I'm leaving now, darling. I shall mail the divorce papers to you. Please be well, and know that I shall always think of you fondly." And she left.

The next few months were full of telephone calls and apartment searches, and then life settled into its new, lovely routine. She took long baths with an almost unseemly amount of water and dried herself off with towels that felt wickedly decadent.

One evening she stepped off of the subway, and saw that same man staring at the skyline. She stood beside him, shading her eyes with her gloved hand to see what he saw.

"This city, it's so extraordinary," he said to her. He didn't pull his gaze from the brick buildings. "I could watch it all day. So much life, so much beauty."

She saw it, felt the life of the city running through her veins in a way that she had never understood before. Being so close to a person in love...well, it must have a way of rubbing off on you, she thought.

"Look at that window there," she said, and pointed. "I imagine that there is a lovely woman inside, playing the piano. Do you know why I think this? Look at the way the sun is hitting that particular window. It's making rainbows there, but not on any of the others. That window is a place where magic happens."

The man tilted his head for a second, pondering the window, and then he turned to look, really *look* at her.

She nodded her head once, for yes, this was just right, and then her heels tapped smartly away. She felt him watching her until she was out of sight.

MUSIC TO JUMP BY

The first time that I saw him, Vel had no bones. He lounged on the chair like he was melting into it, and I came to learn that was the way he always was. He watched the room with dark eyes that seemed half closed and lazy, but were really alert and bright. Not that anybody would know this.

Vel undraped himself from the chair and walked my way. I stood in the doorway, peering into the dark room, my eyes still adjusting to the lack of light.

"It's okay to come inside," he said, and reached out his hand.

I hesitantly took it, and his skeleton felt firm and strangely cool under his skin. And really, that's where it all began.

Vel was my boyfriend's roommate at the time, and even after the breakup, Vel and I remained close. He'd swing by at night, letting himself in through the upstairs window that never quite shut all of the way. This never bothered me. He was constantly burning his CDs, making eclectic new mixes for every occasion. *Music for the Sea*, for example, and *Boring Songs for Lame Weddings*. I especially loved his *Music to Drive the Neighbors Mad* mix; it was spectacularly loud with a gritty beat. Vel was a genius.

But he was unpredictable, and sometimes that made him scary.

"Vel," I said, and shook his shoulder gently. He had fallen asleep on my bed while I was out getting groceries. He didn't move.

"Vel!"

"Go away."

His voice was very low and already sounded dangerous, but I didn't have the patience to deal with it right then.

"You have to wake up."

He raised his head and the look in his eyes made me take a step back, snatching my hand away.

"I said, go away."

And I did. Simple as that. He gets like that sometimes, and it was far better just to back off instead of trying to bully him out of it. After making dinner, I tiptoed upstairs to see if he wanted any, but he had already left through the window. This didn't surprise me.

One day he slipped a CD into my hands. He held it a little too long, a little too delicately, and the back of my head tingled. I knew there was something important about it.

"What's this?" I asked, turning it over in my hands. There was no title, no table of contents. Except for the gentle way he ran his finger down the plastic before handing it over, it could have been just any blank CD in a generic case.

"Nothing special," he said.

"You're lying."

He grinned, and it both warmed and chilled me at the same time.

"Keep a hold of it, will you?"

That night, I slipped it into my player and sat on the corner of my bed in the dark, hugging my pillow and listening to the music. It was even more eclectic than usual, but most of the songs were familiar. There were songs sung by children, and ones with heavy, driving beats. One that was tragically ethereal, and another in Russian that I had never heard before. He had dedicated a song to me once, slow and nonsensical, and that was on there as well. I turned it off and leaned back against the headboard. I just needed to think for a while. It was as if a single life was being played out on that CD. A soundtrack, perhaps. I wondered if it was the soundtrack to Vel.

The next day I stopped by his apartment.

"Tell me what this is," I demanded, throwing the CD onto the couch.

He looked at it with his lazy eyes, and then directly at my face. "It's a CD."

"Obviously. Tell me what you made it for." I was nervous, and being nervous made me angry. I shoved my hands into my pockets so he wouldn't see them shaking.

He noticed this, then shrugged his shoulders and lolled his head over the back of the couch. He stared at the ceiling for a long time. A fly buzzed past his ear, but he didn't even blink.

"Vel. Don't ignore me."

His sigh was gentle, but I heard the exasperation and the weariness in it.

"It's not for anything, okay? It's just to...enjoy. So enjoy it."

Without looking, he scooped up the CD and flung it back at me. I couldn't catch it on time. The case opened and the CD spilled out, hitting the floor with a sound that reminded me of broken eggs and car crashes. I fell to my knees, picking the disc up and running my fingers over the new, raw scratches. I felt strangely close to crying.

"You're sure you're okay?" I asked. I bit my lip. "I kind of wondered if you had made it to be the soundtrack of your life. And then I wondered why you would feel the need to do that." I couldn't look directly at him, and shifted my gaze to somewhere off to his left.

Out of the corner of my eye, I saw him grin. "The soundtrack of my life, huh? I like that. If only I could be so lucky."

He seemed a bit happier after that, but only barely. Happiness for Vel was that elusive thing that never quite came to pass. He told me once that he was content with the shadows of other people's happiness. That was why he hung out with me, I think. There were enough shadows to go around.

But he started disappearing more often. He'd drive his car to the top of the cliffs, sitting on the hood and staring at the ocean. It was a pretty dangerous area, really, and had been fenced off a long time ago, but the fences had long since been torn down by the local kids.

I used to go with him, every now and then, but lately I had the feeling that my company wouldn't be tolerated, let alone appreciated. I'd just watch Vel stare down at the thrashing water, and I didn't want to do that. It was like watching his soul slip away, and not being able to do anything about it. A soul is a soft, indefinable thing, but the feeling of it sliding through your fingertips is unmistakable. I feared this.

I think he knew it. But there wasn't anything he could do about it, and that was what really frightened me. He couldn't make himself stay, not any more than I could. Each time that I saw him now, I unconsciously clenched my fists, somehow hoping to hold his presence around as long as possible. I saw it in the way his empty eyes traveled over my face and hair and then toward the sky. He was already disappearing.

"Come out to the cliffs," he said. "And bring the CD."

I tossed his mix in the passenger side of my truck and drove up the winding path to his spot. The sun would be going down soon. The thought felt ominous.

Vel was where I knew he would be, cross legged on the hood of his car. He barely glanced my way when he heard my footsteps, but that small sign of greeting was enough.

"Put it in, would you?"

I slid into the driver's side and fed the CD into the player. I turned the volume up, and hopped on the hood next to Vel.

The music poured out around us, and Vel closed his eyes and leaned back.

"Let's just listen for a while," he said.

It was hard to breathe. I leaned back on the windshield next to him, and we both stared at the sky, the pink-orange of sunset streaking across the clouds. Vel reached for my hand, and I held it tightly. His fingers were relaxed and cool.

"Do you want to dance?" he asked, pulling me off of the hood.

There was something terrifying about this dance. He held me too close, and I stared wildly over his shoulder while he hummed, dragging me around through the sharp rocks and pieces of old seashells. The driving beat of his CD changed to something young and light, and then to something painfully ancient and angry. The inappropriateness of the music made the dance seem even more bizarre.

He dipped me once, and I realized just how close we were to the edge.

"Vel, stop it!" I pulled back, but he wouldn't release me from his arms. I didn't think that I wanted him to, anyway. I tried to imagine myself as something tall and stable for him, but I felt how wispy my spirit really was.

"Please," I pleaded. I felt my eyes burn. "Please, let's back away from the edge."

He didn't move, just hummed with the CD. His eyes were seeing far beyond me now. I felt my hands fall loosely at my sides. It was like I couldn't control them.

"Look at me. Look at me!"

He finally focused on my mouth, concentrating on what I was saying. I enunciated as clearly as I could.

"I don't want to watch you jump."

His smile was warm, and made it all the way up to his eyes. He put his hand on my face and started waltzing me around again. I wasn't nearly as clumsy this time.

"You could come with me, you know."

He didn't miss a step as he said it, just swung me around and spun me under his arm. The music was playing a wild, broken tune that reminded me of Old Norse battles.

"I...I don't think I want to."

"But we're meant to be together, you and I." Vel swayed his head with the music, and suddenly I felt like twirling, so I did. His smile was more beautiful than the stars. "Nobody understands me like you do." The surreal quality of it all was making me light headed. Look at us, I thought. Waltzing to The Mickey Mouse Club on these cliffs. Just *look*.

Vel was singing, "You and me, you and me, into the sea..." and laughed so hard that he nearly doubled over. He was happier than I had seen in a long time. The setting sun streaked his hair with pink.

"The sun is going down," I said.

He nodded. "It is."

The music changed to something soft and innocent, with just a hint of sadness behind it.

"This is my favorite song," I said, surprised. I hadn't noticed it on the mix before.

"I know." The humor had gone completely out of Vel's voice, and he stopped dancing. He stepped closer to the edge and pulled me with him. He slid his arms around me, his touch butterfly soft, and studied me very seriously.

I looked down the cliffs at the sea below, and then back at my truck, and finally at Vel. "I think I hate you for this," I said.

He didn't even blink. "No, you don't."

And smiled.

AXES

She seemed like such a nice girl, so the whole "being an axe murderer" thing was pretty hard to handle. She was so squeamish. She didn't even like to touch raw meat. Naturally I was pretty surprised when I ran down the cellar steps and saw her dismembering the cat lady from next door with an axe.

"Whoa," I said. That was my first mistake.

Jill whirled around, her huge axe shining in the dim light.

"Cripes, Jill, it's me! Don't mow me down!" I ducked to one side, holding an oversized package of pork loins in front of my face as a shield. Jill's axe dropped a bit, hovered, and then dropped a bit more.

"What are you doing down here?" she asked me. She had blood smeared across the front of her party dress and above her upper lip. I politely tried not to stare.

"Not much," I said, feigning calmness. "I'm just here to stick this meat in the freezer. We'll never get to it before it turns."

"No!" she said, and held out her hand, but I had already yanked the freezer door open.

That was my second mistake.

I shrieked and slammed the heavy door down again, but it was too late. I had already seen bits and pieces of random people tossed casually inside.

"Was that the creepy guy from the video store?" I turned to Jill, but all I saw was the subtle shine as something came swinging my way.

She clocked me with the flat of the axe. Just like that. I woke up to find myself sitting ingloriously on my butt, my back against the freezer and my arms chained awkwardly.

"Feeling better?" Jill asked me with genuine concern.

"Sure, thanks."

"No problem."

Jill was still hacking away at the cat lady. She seemed to be having a hard time pulling the joints apart. Something kept sticking.

"Is that tendon?" I asked her, curious.

"I'm not sure. It's something, though." She started using the axe like a crowbar, and threw her weight against it. I bit my lip.

"It's not coming apart very neatly, is it?"

"Stop criticizing me!" Jill leaned on the axe and glared at me.

"I'm not criticizing, Jilly! I'm just trying to be..." I dunno. Helpful. My mama had taught me right.

"The others weren't this much trouble," she confided, and popped her back. Her beautiful blonde hair was falling out of its careful chignon.

Some girls have all the luck. And apparently that girl wasn't me.

"I'm going to have to kill you now," Jill told me.

"Why?" I fairly wailed. I couldn't help it. She was really wrecking my day.

"Well, now you know. That I kill people. Mostly on the weekends, originally, but now I've learned how to fit it into my schedule better. Organization is such a pain."

This was totally absurd. I mean, she couldn't shake season salt on raw *chicken*, for crying out loud, but she could manage to dismember people? And more to the point, she could manage to dismember *me*?

"I thought we were friends," I burbled. Tears were squeezing themselves out of my eyes. And my skirt was riding up, big time. I was wearing yellow monkey underwear, and this was how they were going to find me. I tried to wipe my nose on my shoulder.

"Man, you're pathetic," she said. This really ticked me off.

"What, somehow you'd manage to be all stoic? You're one sick puppy, Jill, do you know that?" I lunged toward her a few times, but the chains held fast.

"I'm sorry about this," she said. "I really am. I like you." Jill shrugged. "But you know how it goes."

I struggled against the chains again. "No, I do not know how it goes! Jeez, Jill! Let me go."

Jill shook her head. "I can't. You'll get me in trouble, and my mom would kill me. Goodbye college fund, goodbye new car."

I couldn't help it. I goggled. "You are so selfish."

Oops. Wrong thing to say. Jill's brown eyes narrowed.

"You were always such a brat. I could have killed you a million times over by now." She took a mighty swing with her axe and the cat lady's legs severed neatly from her hips. "Finally. It's about time something goes my way."

Her phone rang. Jill automatically reached for it, but her eyes clashed with mine.

"I'll get this upstairs," she said, and scurried up and out of the basement. I heard the door slam above me.

This was my chance. I tried to ignore the decapitated heads and sloppily butchered body parts that littered the cellar. I couldn't believe that girl! Making me slice and stuff all of the pork chops because they felt slimy to her. What about that head over there? Didn't that freak her out? I wriggled and shimmied and tried to extricate myself from the chains that were holding me to the freezer. Stupid freezer. I wish I'd never seen the thing.

"Sucks to be you," said a voice out of the darkness.

I jumped so hard that I slammed the back of my head against the freezer. The pupils of my eyes felt like stars, and I ran my tongue over my teeth to make sure that they hadn't been rattled out.

"Hmm. Can't say that wasn't satisfying."

I blinked a few times, and turned my head toward the familiar voice.

"What are you doing here?" I asked. I really didn't want to hear the answer.

"Why, my love, what a silly question. I'm here...for you."

He drifted my way, his black cloak spilling around him like fog. His hood was pulled low over his face, but I could still see the glitter of his eyes. He stretched out his arm and pointed at me with fingers of exposed bone.

"I have come to take you home," Death said. And smiled.

"Knock it off, Death. Get me out of here!" I rattled my chains at him, and his smile widened.

"I don't wanna," he said, and sat down next to me. He looked around the room and whistled. "Jill's some piece of work. Bet you're regretting kicking me out of the house now, aren't you?" He picked up a severed arm and examined it.

"This so isn't the time to talk about this, Death! Release me before she comes back!" I gave him my most commanding glare, but he didn't seem to notice.

"Poor me, booted out of my home and forced to find new lodgings elsewhere. And you, you shack up with a psycho killer. *Qu'est-ce que c'est?*" He started to hum, and patted me on the shoulder with the detached hand.

"Please," I said, giving up. "I don't want to die."

Death lowered his head and looked at me from under the hood. "You're going to have to, you know. Everybody does."

I went cold. "Now?"

Death stared at me for a long time, and I stared back in horror. Finally he sighed. "No, not now. I guess. Man, I am such a softie." He stood up, and tossed the arm into the corner. It landed with a wet thump. "But we have to establish some rules."

"Like what?"

Death paced around the cellar room, ticking the rules off on his fingers. "Number one, I get to move back in. I hate my new roommate. He's such a dweeb."

"I...okay. But you can't leave your beetles and things around the living room. It's so disconcerting," I pointed out, when he turned to glare at me.

"I don't think you have much room to negotiate, pretty girl."

He was right. We'd talk about this later. "Anything else?"

"Rule number two. You know that twenty bucks that I owe you?"

I nodded my head. "Yeah."

"Debt forgiven. Got it?"

I nodded again. My life for twenty bucks? Freakin' steal, I say! Suddenly I heard the basement door open, and my mouth went dry.

"Death, hurry! She's on her way down!"

"One more thing," he said, and I began to panic. I scrabbled at the chains and heard a strange mewling sound. It took a second to realize that it was coming from me.

"Calm down!" he ordered, and the authority in his voice shut me up. For the first time I saw Death as somebody to fear instead of the gangly sack of bones who ate all of my Cheetos and saved over my games on the Playstation. I stared at him with wide eyes.

"What else do you want?" I whispered.

Death looked at me and grinned, his skull shining in the dim light. "That's for me to know and you to find out."

I scowled and he shrugged. "I haven't decided yet. But I'll let you know when I do. Now hush."

And hush I did. Jill had descended the stairs and stood staring at us.

"So, you're Death," she said. She sounded strangely unfazed. That's because she's totally a creepy psycho weirdo, I decided. I have the worst luck in roommates.

"I am," Death said. His cloak was swaying around him in an extra ghostly way. Sometimes that guy knows how to work the ambiance.

"Funny. I never saw you when I killed anybody else." Jill looked equally excited and annoyed.

Death shrugged. "I show myself to whomever I choose." Man, he was being suave today. Jill looked ready to pounce on him and drag him off to the Tunnel of Love.

"And you choose to show yourself to me?" Jill batted her eyes.

I turned to her in surprise. "You're so flirting with him! You're flirting with Death! My gosh, woman!"

Jilly grabbed the axe from the ground and pointed it at me. "Shut up!" She swung it high over her head, but Death gently took it from her. He set it back on the ground, blade up. Jill looked confused.

"I thought that you were here because I was going to kill her," she said.

"That's why I came, yes," Death told her. He took both of her hands in his. She didn't flinch at the feel of cold bone.

"So why won't you let me?" she asked.

Death shook his head almost angrily. "It would happen this way."

I felt my nerves start up again. What, he was going to let me die just because Jilly was *crushing* on him?! This was so unfair!

I was just about to launch into an angry tirade voicing my opinion when Death stood perfectly straight and still. Darkness flowed into the room, and creepy little things chittered and scampered in the corners.

"Wow," breathed Jill, looking around.

"Yeah, wow," Death said, and then he touched Jill right between the eyes with his skeletal finger. Jill jerked and fell backwards.

Onto the axe.

"Well, there you go," Death said cheerfully. The darkness subsided and he gave me a little wink. "I'll start moving my stuff in."

I fought the chains. "But you can't leave me here!" Dead cat lady. Dead Jilly. Dead creepy video store guy. And those were just the ones I knew about.

"Take me with you!" I screamed.

Death started for the stairs. "As much as I love to hear you say that, it's not practical. What are you going to say? That Death unchained you? Come on. Scream until somebody finds you and then tell them that you kicked your roomie onto the axe. You'll be fine."

"Death, you get back here right now!" I yelled. I could have killed him. Seriously.

"That's good. Keep that up, love. See you when the police find you," he said, and then Death was gone.

The bodies, however, weren't.

So I took his advice. I kept screaming.

THE QUIET PLACES WHERE YOUR BODY GROWS

Azhar's little girl was found slowly, laboriously, in pieces. Her feet were flashing like diamonds in the creek. Tiny hands were strung from the stubby branch of the Crying Trees. Her head, eyes dark and her black pigtails shorn, was left in a field where curious wildflowers bent into her mouth. The torso was never discovered.

Azhar had terrible dreams about what happened to his daughter's young, dusky body, of what became of her heart. In the dreams, he stood playing a flashlight over the corpse of his sweet Sada while lightning splintered on the bleak horizon. Sometimes there was a monster. Sometimes there was a man. Sometimes he himself knelt down and ripped out his own daughter's organs with his teeth. He was a man who had become a monster.

He hoped they were only dreams.

This was normal, his best friend at home said. Transference of guilt. Agony of a father who couldn't protect his little one when she needed him most.

"I told her that monsters didn't exist," Azhar explained to his friend over the phone. "I lied."

"Everybody tells their children that monsters don't exist." His friend's voice was kind. They had known each other since they were infants. They had kicked a red ball in the dirt until it was stained and worn so thin that it had no choice but to deflate. His daughter had also been used until her skin could no longer contain her insides.

"I lied," Azhar repeated. He hung up the phone and never dialed that number again.

America was a large land, a land where one could get lost. He lost his native dress, he lost his heart to a beautiful American woman, and he lost the hard edges of his accent. But he could never lose the memories of Sada's white, milk-fed teeth and strong, coltish legs.

He wondered if his baby's killer thought the same thing.

"He was very handsome," Sada told him in his dreams that evening. She was standing in a rain so cold that he would be able to see her breath if she had been breathing. "He looked like a prince, not a butcher. Have you ever seen a prince, Daddy?"

He had not.

"Maybe princes aren't real," Sada said. Her eyes were crafty and sad at the same time. "But monsters are." She opened her mouth wide and showed Azhar the wildflowers sitting on her tongue.

The Handsome Butcher liked stealing little girls and boys. They were found hanging from trees and tucked into suitcases like tiny gifts. One child, at first, and then two. A dozen. Two dozen. The community became aware that children don't line up neatly like toy soldiers when you call them; they dart like rabbits through burrows. They fly like starlings through the air. They dance like wisps of paper in a flame and then they flutter away, pieces of darling ash, and they land where whimsy takes them. If you are lucky, that means they will gently settle into their beds at night, faces washed and teeth brushed. If you are unlucky, they will land in the fingers of bad men. These fingers twist and pluck and slice. These fingers hurt.

Azhar didn't want to ask Sada what happened. He didn't want to know. But she told him, her delicate, piano-note voice hitting ugly chords while she talked.

"No more," he begged. Tears made his lashes even darker. "I can't hear anymore."

Sada sighed, looked at the sky. "I miss my dolly. And I'm always hungry."

Two towns over, another little girl went missing. She, too, was stolen from her bed. She also had pigtails like banners. The police had no suspects at this time, they said, but Azhar knew it was The Handsome Butcher. He and this frantic mother shared something. Loss. The grief. Perhaps their girls could be friends on the other side.

"I won't give up hope," the mother said firmly into television cameras. There was something scary in her eyes, that same determination that Azhar had worn until pieces of Sada were found. "I'll find her and then I'll kill whoever stole her from me."

Azhar understood. He spent long hours sitting in the field where Sada's beautiful face once rested. The wind, the wildflowers. How could a place of beauty survive such loss? Greenery growing over the horrors. Misery soaked up by grasses.

He took a picture one day. Of the meadow. Of the creek and the terrible Crying Trees. They were perfect on film. Places of peace. When Azhar saw the pictures, he was haunted by Sada, but he was the only one. Others thought they were beautiful. Others who didn't know.

These, he silently told his daughter, *these are the quiet places where your body grows.*

He tucked the pictures into his wallet. He would show the mother from two towns over. Show her that there is a semblance of life After. When her little one turns up in pieces like his did, she'll collapse and that will be okay. But After, she'll be able to see the beauty in the land again. If she just looks hard enough. If she just keeps the dreams at bay.

"I love you, Daddy," Sada whispered that night. She was forced to whisper because her throat was rotting out. Azhar turned on his side and looked at his pictures of peace.

"We'll make it through this," he said. He wasn't quite certain who he was talking to, but the words seemed exactly right.

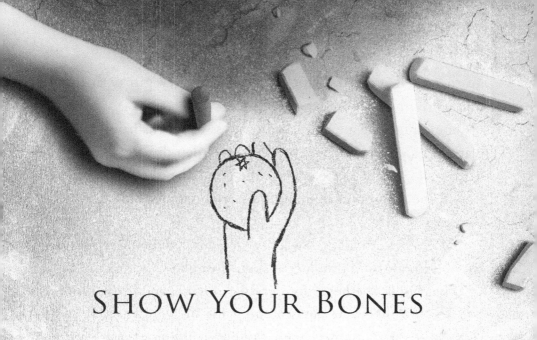

SHOW YOUR BONES

She stopped eating at nineteen. One day she simply pushed her plate away, and got up from her lonely dinner table outside in the sun. That was that. Her father never noticed, not with her girlhood friends parading in and out of the mansion. She would listen to the squeaking of springs at night and wish that she could throw up. Sometimes, with a little help, she did.

Some days she would take an orange from the concerned cook and walk with it to the pond in the middle of the gardens. She would peel it and sniff at the rind, watching the juice run down her arm before tossing it to the goldfish. Her hair thinned and began to fall out; she cropped it short in a sophisticated hairstyle that, after being published in the magazines, had hordes of others flocking to the salons to achieve the same effect. When her skin blanched, she left it, not attempting to tint it with colored plaster and caked crayons like other women. "Beautiful," they breathed, and in the next issue of *Beauty Magazine*, tender, pale faces gazed alluringly at the camera.

When her collarbones and hipbones jutted out, instantly the world began to diet, coveting that brittle look. "Gorgeous," her father grinned, and winked, before leading a hungry girl with carefully tousled short hair upstairs to his room.

Sometimes she ate a little bit of grass or thorns from the garden plants, or she chewed on a handful of garden dirt for the nutrients. Mostly she just sat at the edge of the pond, dangling her bare white legs in the water and thinking quietly about anything but food. It wasn't at all hard.

"You're breathtaking, Sweetie," her father said one day, admiring her cheekbones and translucent skin. "Just like your mother."

That night, she heard him crying upstairs, and it took him two hours before he went out searching for his woman. She was left alone in the garden once again, holding handfuls of dark earth. She cupped her hands together like she was bearing the world between them, the moon glistening and reflecting on the grains of mica and quartz. She stared at it for a long time, her lips nibbling at the air just above it, before letting it all slip through her fingers.

She wiped her hands on her white dress and walked away.

THE ABCS OF MURDER

I got really tired of murdering Billy Cords.

I know how that sounds, but I can't help it. I'm a peaceful guy at heart, and the constant scheming and planning and carrying out murder after murder was really getting to me. To be honest, I'd rather be playing basketball. And I hate basketball.

Besides, Billy was my best friend, a fact that he kept bringing up.

"Hey, loser," he said, popping up at the foot of my bed one evening. I sat up, clutching my bed sheet and screaming. This was most likely because we had buried Billy two days earlier.

"Cripes, Jake, knock it off." He covered his ears and bared his teeth. This was such a Billy move that it only made me scream harder. I heard pounding feet come tearing down the hall. Billy sighed and slid under my bed. My father flew into the room, wearing his boxers and wielding a golf club like a weapon. The way that my father played, that was most likely the case.

"What's wrong?" He sidled up to the window and peeked outside. I had stopped screaming and was hunched over, openmouthed. My dad looked at me.

"You look as if you've seen a ghost, son." I winced. That line was so clichéd, I was embarrassed. Under the bed I heard a muffled snerk. Billy was trying his best to keep himself under control.

"Dad, it was Billy. I saw Billy, he was right at the foot of my bed and—"

Dad sat down, and his face was sad. He ran his hand over his balding head.

"Jake," he said, and didn't seem to know what to say after that. I looked at him, waiting. I heard Billy squirm under the bed a bit and I felt the same way. Dad had acted like this when Mom died, and it was awkward enough the first time.

My father swooped me into his arms for a punishing hug. I struggled, but he held me fast and used his chin to hold my shoulder in place. "I love you, son," he said with feeling, and hugged me even tighter. I let myself go loose in his grip. Kinda like playing dead, but a little bit smarter.

"I...love you too, Dad," I said. My eyes narrowed as I heard another giggle from Billy, but I was sure that Dad didn't pick up on it. On account of his sobbing.

"I don't know what to do for you, boy. Losing Billy. You're going to see him everywhere, that's the way of it. Behind corners and in crowds and picking green olives out at the grocery store. But he's gone, and you're going to have to accept it, although you can talk to him whenever you're lonely and..."

I kinda tuned out, then. It's not that I didn't appreciate my dad and this unusual display of affection, but come on. Plus my dead best friend was getting all restless under the bed. He didn't have an awful lot of patience. ADD, practically. I knew it was time for this craziness to end.

"Boy, Dad, thanks a lot," I interrupted, and then I faked a big, jaw-cracking yawn. "And I sure am tired. Big test tomorrow, and all that." I smiled sweetly. A bit too sweetly, actually, but Dad was relieved enough to cut his parenting short.

"Sleep well, son," he said, and hovered his face around my head for an instant. I was afraid that he was going to go in for a kiss like I was ten years old or something, but instead he just mussed up my hair and left the room, taking the golf club with him.

"That was close," Billy said, sliding out from under my bed.

I just stared at him.

"What?" he said.

"What do you mean *what*? You're dead!" I climbed out of bed and smacked his arm. There was a little resistance there, but not much, and my hand went all of the way through pretty easily.

"Ow!" Billy yowled, jerking his arm away.

"What, that hurt?" I asked. A little hopefully, I had to admit. If he was going to scare me so bad, then he at least ought to get a slap out of it. It's just the way our relationship always went.

"Nah, it doesn't hurt. Just kidding ya. Hey, Jake," he said, and suddenly his brown eyes were very serious. "I need your help with something. As you can see, something's not right."

"What do you need?" It was a simple question, but I wasn't prepared for the answer or the look on his face when he answered.

"I need you to kill me."

"I can't do this," I told him the next morning. We were standing behind my house. I was holding the wood axe in my hand like it had been dipped in poison. Something gross and acidic was in my mouth. This was so uncool.

"Dude, I told you I can't feel anything," Billy said. He was sounding ticked off. "Just do it already!" He closed his eyes and turned his face away.

"Billy," I said. I was speaking very calmly so that he could understand me. I heard that's what you're supposed to do with crazy people. "I don't want to kill you in the first place. I mean, what's so bad about being a ghost? I know," I said when he angrily opened his mouth, "you said it's boring and you feel like you're not in the right place, but come on! Killing you with an axe? An axe!"

I pointed at the axe with my other hand. Billy didn't look impressed.

"Look, just do it. I can't explain it, but I just need to die, okay? Be a pal."

I sighed and squinched my eyes shut. "You so owe me," I said. I peeked through one eye to make sure that the axe blade would land squarely in his heart, and then I swung with all of my might.

Billy made a strangled gasping sound and then fell to the ground. He disappeared. I left the axe where it was and ran into the bushes, vomiting. It was the worst day of my life.

At least it was until nightfall, when Billy popped over my bed again.

"Didn't work," he said. He shook his head. "We'll have to find another way to do it."

"Billy!" I kept running my hands over where the axe had hit him, but there wasn't a mark, just that same resistance before my hands passed through.

"Dude, you can never ask me to do that again." My hands were shaking. "Do you know what it's like to kill somebody? It's the sickest, heaviest, most repulsive…"

He merely looked at me. "I'm already dead. For the most part. And we're going to try again tomorrow. I need your help, Jake."

So we did.

Nothing worked. We tried poison, guns, knives. I pushed him off of buildings, ran over him with cars and set him on fire. That one almost burned down the shed.

"This sucks," I said, after my father berated me for "acting out." "Dad totally thinks I'm an arsonist. He's getting creeped out seeing me parade in and out of the house with all sorts of different weapons. Obviously this isn't working."

"What about that wrench?" Billy said, perking up. "What if you just, you know, crack me over the head a good one? Think that will work?"

"It's worth a try," I sighed, and *thonked* Billy as hard as I could right over his eye. He jerked, fell backwards, and faded away. I wasn't at all surprised to see him sitting on my bed after I came up from dinner.

"Not wrenches, either." He cursed. "This is taking too long. It's been weeks already."

"Tell me about it," I said, and he opened his eyes wide. "Man, it's giving me nightmares! It's changing the way I'm seeing things, you know. I'm always looking around, wondering exactly how I should go about murdering you. It gets old." I flopped on the bed, and Billy was quiet for a minute. Which was unusual for him.

"So I meant to ask you, how are your college plans coming along?" Billy tried to sound disinterested, like it didn't really matter. College scared the crap out of me, and he knew it. But it's important to Dad, so it's supposed to be important to me.

"Not so well, you know? I signed up to volunteer at the animal shelter, because it'll look good on an application one day. I meant to spend some time out there lately, but I've been kinda busy." If Billy felt guilty, he didn't show it. And I didn't want him to feel guilty, not really. I punched my pillow and Billy looked at me.

"What?" he asked. His eyebrows were arched.

"I don't know. How about…" I went through the options in my head. "What if it has to be something from your house? Something symbolic or something. Could that be the case?"

Billy perked up. "It's worth a try," he said.

After school the next day I stopped off to visit Billy's mom.

"Hi, Rose," I said, hugging her when she opened the door. "How are you holding up?"

Rose's eyes turned wet when she saw me, but her smile didn't tremble at all. "Good," she said, and hugged me back harder than I thought she had strength for. Billy slipped in through the bedroom window while Rose and I were talking. We weren't sure if she'd be able to see him or not, but he didn't want to take the chance.

"You want to go poke around in his room?" Rose offered after a while. "Spend time with Billy's memory? If there's something particularly special to you, feel free to have it. Just run it past me first, will you?"

"Sure thing, Rose," I said, and grinned at her. Rose was good people. Even Billy thought so.

"Go on up, then," she said. Then she looked me dead in the eye. "Sometimes I feel like Billy is still around. You ever get that feeling?"

I swallowed hard, but managed to answer in a clear voice. "That's because he is. He's right here." I gestured vaguely upstairs and Rose smiled.

"You're a good kid, Jakob. Always were. Always will be. You're a credit to your mama, may she rest in peace." She crossed herself with a finger bedecked in rings. Then she went into the kitchen, leaving me to search Billy's room in private.

Billy was leaning by his bedroom door at the top of the stairs. He had been listening.

"Ever check in on your mom?" I asked him, shutting the door. He shook his head and used a sleeve to wipe his eyes. I pretended I was looking elsewhere. Friends do that.

"No," he said finally. "It's too hard." He cleared his throat and began to go through his room, looking for something special and wonderful and mercifully deadly.

"How about this?" I asked, holding up a dragon pewter letter opener. It was shaped like a dagger and dreadfully tacky. We both thought it was pretty cool.

"Maybe. Throw it in the bag. We'll try it later." It was hard to hear his voice because he was rifling through the closet. He emerged and tossed a backpack at me. "Keep these," he said. I knew what it was without looking. The bag had all of his Playstation games, and a couple of the old school NES cartridges. They were gold to me.

"Thanks!" I said, and Billy grinned.

"No problem."

We put together a pretty good stash of murder weapons by the end. We were starting to get creative, using extension cords for hanging and trying to figure out how to electrocute him. I mean, we had to. We were struggling here. Murder for Hire we weren't.

"So what was it like to die?" I asked him. I'd been dying (ha ha) to know, but hadn't brought it up until now.

He stopped flipping through a magazine and stared out of the window.

111

"I don't know," he said slowly. "It wasn't like I thought it would be."

"What do you mean? Like you thought it would be? How would you know that?"

Billy started to grind his molars together, and suddenly I knew that I wouldn't like what he was going to say. Suddenly the bag of video games seemed very interesting.

"When I went out driving that night, I was pretty freaked out. I mean, I was freaked out about graduation, you know. And college. Where I'd end up. I'm not as smart as you..."

He paused, on the verge of shouting. I was surprised at how angry he sounded. Surprised enough to look at him.

Billy took a deep breath and said much more calmly, "I'm not as smart as you. I didn't think we'd end up at the same college. I was freaked about getting a job to put myself through school, wherever it is. And you know how I am with girls."

I snorted. I couldn't help it.

"Exactly," he said, nodding. "And in college there's school and jobs and girls. That's pretty much it, yeah? So while I was driving, I had this thought. Very brief. I thought, *What if I—*"

"No," I said. My eyes felt wide enough that they could fall out of my head. "Don't say it. You didn't."

"I did," Billy said, looking at me. I could tell this was taking all of his courage. "For half of a second, I did. I stomped on the gas and headed for the trees."

I was shaking.

"I think I hate you," I said, and my teeth chattered.

Billy bowed his head, and then he looked up. His eyes were glowing.

"What gives you the right to hate me? I screwed up, okay? All of a sudden I came to my senses and I jerked the car back onto the road, but I jerked it too far. The car's spinning, and you know what? It's surreal. It's like a ride. And I'm sitting there thinking, 'Wow, this is fun, I bet Jake would love this' and then it's all *over*. It's *over* and I'm sitting there alone without my frickin' body and I need to die and kill me kill me *kill me kill me!*"

He was screaming at the top of his lungs, and, I realized, so was I. I pushed him down onto the floor and sat on top of him. I wrapped my hands around his throat and pushed down and squeezed as hard as I could. That familiar resistance, but I was stronger than that, I could press harder than that, and I was yelling and crying and my sweat and tears were dropping down onto his face. Billy was gasping, but I didn't care. I'd already killed him a million times by now. I squeezed until his eyes changed and he faded away, but I didn't move. I crouched over where he had been, my hands clawed and ready to squeeze if he came back. He didn't.

Eventually I pushed the hair out of my eyes and took the bag of games. I didn't touch the bag of weapons. I wanted nothing to do with them. I wiped my sweaty palm on my pants. I didn't need weapons, anyway.

Downstairs, Rose greeted me with a knowing glance.

"May I have his games, Rose?" I asked in a voice that didn't sound at all like mine. I was surprised when Rose brushed tears off of my face. I had thought I'd stopped crying long ago.

"Of course you may, dear," she said. I was prepared to apologize for the screaming that she had heard, but she simply never asked. Maybe she had covered her ears and turned away from the sound. Perhaps she had done the same thing in his room late at night.

Billy didn't show up in my room again. I don't exactly know why that is. Maybe it's because I killed him in anger with my bare hands. Or maybe it's because now I know the truth. That he was frightened. That he screwed up. Maybe it's because it turned out that we were both killers.

My dad is relieved now. No longer does he have to watch me throwing axes in the backyard. No more seeing me with guns and nooses made out of shoelaces and setting the shed on fire, screaming at myself. No more saying a prayer and locking his bedroom door against me at night, just in case, his trusty golf club by his side.

"I'm glad everything's back to normal, Jake," he told me. "You don't know what a relief it is." He turned to me, and I had to look away from his sincerity. "I know that Billy's death has been hard for you, and things were rough for a while. But you're coming out of this just fine. Something like this, and the way that you act under stress...well, it shows you just what kind of a person you really are."

I glanced down at my killing hands, which were curled into fists.

Yeah. That's exactly what I'm afraid of.

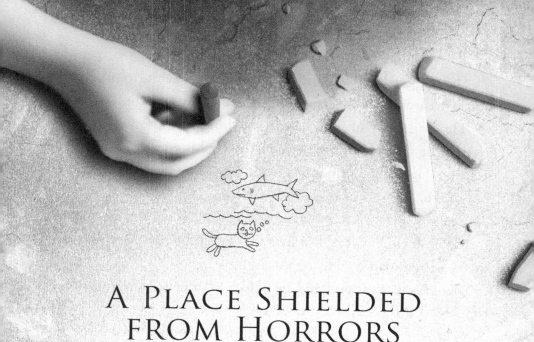

A PLACE SHIELDED
FROM HORRORS

She carried a basket of warm muffins. They smelled of orange and lemon and had a rich, crumbly topping made out of brown sugar. She tripped over something on the floor and nearly dropped the basket. It was the tiger shark. He turned his head and growled at her, nipping at her ankles.

"Toby, no biting," she said firmly, and tapped the shark's blunt nose with the toe of her slipper. The shark snorted and swam across the carpet.

She had been here for days. Days and days, or even weeks. Months, perhaps, or as long as a year. She couldn't tell. It was a beautiful place without windows. A home with a single door that assembled itself together like a puzzle made of different types of wood.

An orange puff meowed and clawed at her skirt. She set the muffins down on a table made of bone and picked up a green-eyed cat. He purred.

"How are you, my lovely, my perfect one?" The cat pushed his head into her neck, kneaded his paws into her shoulder. I love you, I love you, he told her silently. She understood.

She hugged him back and took him to the Water Room. Keeping her feet carefully away from the edge, she tossed the cat into the air. He sang a joyful note before splashing into the water, zipping around the floating furniture and stroking his way even deeper into nothing. His happy sounds created bubbles that floated to the surface and broke.

There was a knock at the door. Surprised, the girl danced over to answer it. It took several minutes to disassemble the door enough so a dark haired man could step through.

His hair was mussed and he held a bouquet of singing flowers. He peered at the girl with raised eyebrows.

"Perhaps I am lost?" he said almost hopefully. Toby the tiger shark prowled over to inspect him. He rubbed against the man's leg several times, his rough skin fraying the corduroy of his pants. The man patted the shark's dorsal fin absently, and Toby slid away from his hand.

"Perhaps," the girl agreed. The flowers had their heads together like an old barbershop quartet. The man looked at them again and handed the bouquet to the girl. She accepted it graciously. The flowers applauded themselves and began a new song, something melancholy.

"How about something with more pep?" asked the girl, and the flowers switched to an old June Christy song.

"Lovely," praised the girl, and the flowers beamed.

"Anyway," she said to the handsome, dark-haired man, "what brings you here. Can I help you in some way?"

His head swiveled as he studied the room. "I've never seen a place quite like this. It's extraordinary." His gaze settled on the girl, whose hair floated around her face as though she were underwater. She smiled at him.

"It is quite wonderful," she agreed. "Although I do get lonely. I was forgotten here, you see. I had a friend who used to visit quite often, but that was so very long ago. Perhaps he has changed, and I haven't, and I will wander around this eccentric apartment reading poetry and evading the sun and keeping the horrors away from those who can't do it themselves. I suppose this is loss. I wonder if I should be sad."

The man didn't have an answer for her, but he studied her face with eyes too serious and too angry for someone so young. The girl didn't blush under his analytical gaze, but watched him carefully, and her smile grew even wider inside her heart.

"Ah, you have seen many horrors," she said knowingly. The man nodded gravely, and didn't flinch when she reached for his hand.

"Then that is why you are here," she told him, and led him through the apartment. He wrapped his fingers around hers carefully, and listened as she spoke. "Don't mind Toby; he's a bit of a pest. I have a cat who loves to swim. He's always in this room. Do you care for sweets? I have some fresh muffins, if you'd like one." She chattered away and he listened, a stranger in a place shielded from horrors, his empty shoes left by the door, already being mauled by a curious tiger shark.

LIKE THE STARS

He notices when she enters the room. He can't help but imagine her dress puddling around her feet. He knows that when he looks into her eyes, he will see violets and guillotines. He knows that she will have would-be suitors and would-be murderers after her with just a glance.

She gently touches his shoulder.

"Excuse me," she says. "Would you be able to walk me to my car? It's very dark tonight, and I need a sturdy hand to help me."

He pauses, his calzone partway to his mouth.

"I'd be willing to pay you," she says softly.

No, no, he insists, he'd gladly help her! She wouldn't have to pay a thing.

"Nothing is for free," she says. "Everything has a price, that's the deal." She smiles.

Like the stars, her teeth come out at night.

CROSSWISE COSMOS SABOTAGE

I am standing in the backyard wearing a red shirtwaist dress and heels like it's the 1950s. I'm spraying something with the hose. It's my son.

"He likes it," I tell my neighbors, who are staring at me over the fence. My son is hunched over with his hands covering his head. "It sounds like he's crying, but really he's laughing."

It doesn't matter what I say; my neighbor doesn't speak much English. I hear him chattering to his wife as soon as he's inside the sliding glass door. Maybe one of these days he'll actually close it.

"Okay, that's enough," I say, and turn off the hose. My son raises his face to me, water running into his eyes. "Maybe Daddy will hose you down after work tonight." I coil the hose neatly, ignoring my child as he throws himself backward on the ground. The grass is lush. He won't hurt himself. The neighbor's wife rushes to her window to peek at us. I smile brightly and wave, walking across the lawn on my tiptoes so my heels don't sink into the grass. She disappears behind the curtains. My son is still screaming. I step inside my house, kick off my shoes, and slide the door closed. It dims the sound a little.

The doorbell rings, and I'm surprised. It's the bug guy.

"I thought you were coming on Thursday," I say.

"Nope, Tuesday."

I don't care; I'm just happy to see him. He's letting the cool air out, so I take him by the sleeve and pull him inside. My daughter crawls over and grabs onto my skirt. I pick her up.

"What do you have?" The bug guy asks. He's young and pretty. He has huge plugs in his ears, and although I don't usually like that sort of thing, I like it on him. They say: "Hey, I'm not going to be a bug man forever. I'm going to be Rob Thomas." It's oddly endearing. My daughter reaches for his white work coat, and I switch her to the other hip.

"Cockroaches," I say. "Big ones. Everywhere." I tell him one crawled across the small of my back while I was sleeping the other day. I had been all curled into a ball. I tell him they could be a viable, renewable source of food if we could all just get over the *yick* factor. They live through anything.

"Not this stuff," he says, and goes to work. "When this activates, they're going to want to bail, right? But they're all going to *die.*" His obvious joy over their demise makes me happy. Bloodthirsty. My son wanders in, still dripping. He takes one look at the bug guy and cries.

The bug guy looks at me.

"He doesn't understand," I say simply. The bug guy nods. I smile and call my son into his bedroom to change his clothes.

The doorbell rings again. It's my neighbor from across the street and her terrible child. I want to beat the kid with a hairbrush. Most of us want to, but nobody ever mentions that to his mother.

The boy goes tearing off to cause damage and his mother sighs dramatically and sinks down at the table. "What a stressful day," she says, and lays a hand against her forehead. She spies the bug guy, whistling cheerily as he sprays under the kitchen sink.

"Disgusting. You're *infested*," she says, and shudders exaggeratedly.

I hear something breaking in the back room, and go check. Her son has taken my jewelry box and thrown it into the bathroom sink. I come back to see the mom has my Coke bottle out on the table.

"So let me tell you about this day," she says, and pours Coke into her glass. We both pretend not to notice how much of it she drinks. There won't be any left for my real friend when she comes over, but I don't mind that much. I've decided every sip she takes earns me another iris stolen from her garden.

My daughter pulls the tiny keys off the laptop keyboard and promptly starts choking. I lay her against my shoulder and whack her back until she spits it up on my shoulder. The 'J' key. Always a troublemaker.

There is sobbing from my son's bedroom. The bug guy's spray-gun looks like a giant hypodermic needle. I leave Neighbor and Boy to do as they will, and go check on my little one.

"We'll be in here if you need us," I tell the bug guy, and he nods.

I sit on my son's bed, both kids on my lap. They snuggle against me. I read stories and my neighbor pops in with the phone.

"It's your husband," she says.

I take the phone. "Hi," I say.

"She answered the phone like she lives there," he says.

"It's all part of her plan. Soon she's going to kill me and just move in."

"That would suck. I could never live on a vegetarian diet."

I smile although he can't see me. He knows this, laughs and hangs up.

There's a hesitant knock on the door.

"Come in," I say.

The bug guy opens the door to my son's red and blue bedroom, looks around a little bit. He's cute in the way that small children are cute. Puppies. I want to put him in a box with a warm towel and a hot water bottle.

"Your friend left," he says. "The kid pulled down your blinds in the living room. His mom took a necklace out of that broken box in the sink. I don't think I was supposed to see it."

He holds out the paperwork for me to sign. I pat the bed next to me and he shoves over some stuffed animals and sits down. He's not as scary without his equipment and my kids squirm over to him.

"When I was a kid," I say, "I'd sit on my bed and pretend that it was a boat. I'd take the broom and paddle my way over to Hawaii."

"My bed was always surrounded by molten lava," he says.

I look at the paper again and smile. His name is Billy. I'm not surprised.

"I have a confession to make," he says.

"What?"

"Your friend here asked for some spray to take home. I told her I can't do that, but she kept bugging me. So finally, I gave her a squirt bottle."

"What's wrong with that?" I ask.

"It's full of sugar water."

I laugh, but he still looks worried.

"It's okay," I tell him. My son is trying to look under Billy the Bug Guy's shirt. "For everything she does to me, I pay myself back in flowers from her garden."

"Does she know?"

"Of course not. That would take the sport out of it."

That night I get a phone call. It's my fake neighbor friend.

"There was somebody in my yard," she tells me. "Sneaking around. I think it's a member of a gang."

I don't know what to say to this, but it doesn't matter. She has more to share.

"I have ants," she says. Her voice was trembling with, I want to say rage. "I have never had ants before. Never."

I remember the sugar water and try not to crack up.

"And you have somebody coming up your drive. Somebody in a ball cap. Maybe it's the gang member!"

The doorbell rings.

"He's running away!" she hisses.

"Gotta go," I say, and hang up.

I answer the door. Flowers are strewn all over the porch. Irises, cosmos, daffodils.

"Who is it?" asks my husband, coming up from behind me. The air smells sweet.

"Flowers," I tell him.

"Where'd they come from?"

"The bug guy swiped fake neighbor friend's flowers and then he ran away."

My husband yawns. "Good for him. That took initiative."

I take a flower from the porch and slide it behind my ear. There are enough blooms here to fill the tub.

Maybe I'll do that.

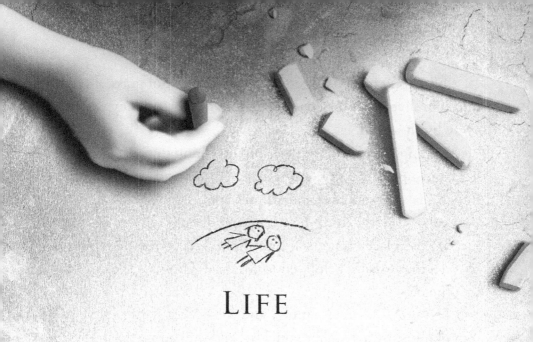

LIFE

Anna lay back in the long grass, staring at the halo around the sun. Her gaze skittered away and landed briefly on a heart-shaped cloud before looking past it into forever.

"It doesn't seem fair," Quit said. He was sprawled out in the grass as well, his head resting on Anna's abdomen. He still had the flowers in his hair that she had braided into it earlier.

"I don't believe that life is meant to be fair," Anna said. She felt the warm weight of his head rise and fall with her breath. The responsibility of it scared her a little, and she watched her stomach go flat, held it there until she gasped again. Quit's brown hair fluttered in the breeze that she created.

"I could love you like my brother does." His voice was surprisingly steady. He had a lighter cadence than Michael Thomas, a much more playful sound.

"Say that again," she commanded. He did.

"You almost sounded like him that time."

"That's not funny, Anna."

"I didn't say it to be funny."

Quit's long brown fingers worked at a piece of grass, shredding it into thin slivers. He tossed them up into the air and they were carried away by the wind.

"A thing of beauty," he said about nothing in particular, and held his hand up to the sky. Anna reached out and grabbed his index finger. He wrapped his hand around hers.

"What do you think he's thinking about right now?" she said, turning their laced fingers into the light. Her foot rested in the patch of grass that usually belonged to Michael Thomas. She wiggled her toes there.

"Dying," Quit said simply, and kissed her hand. His lips left a spot of moisture across her knuckles, and she squinted at it. He began to kiss the tips of her fingers, each one in turn, but she pulled her hand away.

"Stop it," she said, and put her hands over her ears.

"I was just practicing."

Anna ignored him, listening instead to the muffled sound of the wind and the grass through the palms of her hands. Quit began to hum, and turned his face toward her belly. She felt the vibrations through her skin.

With her ears covered, her breathing began to sound very loud. She worked on making it slow and even, lining it up with the beating of her heart. Four beats to every breath in, four beats to every breath out. Like the machines that counted Michael Thomas's breaths.

"He always got to the things that I wanted first," Quit was saying in the background. The way that he shaped his vowels was painfully lovely. "He was always older and faster than I was. He wasn't content to wait for anything. He's probably looking at this as a challenge." He traced lazy circles high on Anna's thigh where her yellow dress had ridden up. She remembered vaguely that she had kicked off her shoes somewhere in the high grass, and couldn't quite remember where they were.   ❧

"I don't think…that I will ever be able to find my car in the parking lot without him," she whispered suddenly. The sun's halo burned in her vision when she closed her eyes. "Michael Thomas always remembers things like that."

Quit ran his hand over her leg like he was erasing something written in the sand. He pulled her hemline down demurely to her knees, smoothed it there.

"I could help you find your car," he said. She shook her head, rustling the grass.

"You get as lost as I do, Quit."

"I could try."

Anna slid out from under him, cozied up to him nose to nose. She ran her hands through his hair, slid them over his cheekbones and rested her thumbs in the hollows beneath. His lashes were wet.

She slipped her knee between both of his, and rested her nose in the hollow of his throat. She felt his pulse jump under her cheek.

"You're alive," she said, and closed her eyes. She felt his shoulder twitch once, and then he stilled. His hand rested on her back. It almost felt like Michael Thomas's hand. She had to say it again.

"You're alive."

LUNA E VOLK

The first time Andros saw her, he knew. He had been raised on tales of the old ways and recognized immediately that there was something more to this girl, something rolling under her skin like the waves of the sea. She was too beautiful; her eyes were too new. She saw magic and wonder in things everybody else took for granted.

"Isn't that stunning?" she said once, studying a tiny white flower that bloomed near a brick wall. The men agreed vocally, as they agreed with everything that she said. The women narrowed their eyes. The girl didn't seem to notice.

"What is your name?" Andros asked her. She straightened and faced him. Starlight shone through her skin.

"I'm Serena. Who are you?"

"Andros," he said. His heart cried out in joy. Serena? Even her name sounded mystical.

"You're not from around here, are you?" he asked knowingly, and Serena laughed.

"Is it that obvious?"

"Maybe not to everyone, but it is to me." He smiled at her, a we're-sharing-a-secret smile, and Serena laughed again.

"You're a strange man, Andros. But I like you."

He liked her too, whoever she was. Wherever she had come from.

He tried to recall everything he could about shape shifters. Was she a skinwalker? He cast the idea aside immediately. Too lovely. Too ephemeral. He felt only lust and desire and his protective instincts rise to the surface when he was around her. No fear. No distrust.

A selkie? A mermaid? Did she come from the sea? This wasn't something he could ask, and she could never tell him; but more than that, he should be able to piece this together on his own.

He asked her out. He rented a canoe and valiantly rowed them around the tiny pond that the city deemed a lake.

"So," he said, panting a little from the exertion, "do you like to swim?"

Serena shuddered delicately. "Oh, goodness, no. I abhor the water. I nearly drowned once when I was a child, and I have been deathly afraid of it ever since."

He stopped rowing and the boat drifted silently.

"But you're here with me," he pointed out. Serena bit her lip and gave a small smile.

"Well, yes. This is where you wanted to come."

"But if you're afraid..."

Her cheeks reddened ever so slightly. "I am afraid. I'm telling myself to be brave, because the water isn't very deep and I believe that you wouldn't let me drown, but I'm still afraid. Yet this is where you wanted to be, and I wanted to be with you."

She turned her face away from him. He studied her dark hair, her pale skin painted with that delicate blush. He suddenly understood what she was trying to say.

"Oh," he said, surprised and delighted.

"Oh," she answered, and covered her face with her hands. Andros leaned forward and took them.

"I would kiss you right now, but I have seen the movies and know that this is when I would upset the canoe. And I never want you to be afraid," he told her.

"How very practical," she agreed, and they both started to laugh. Andros rowed for shore.

She wasn't a selkie. Not a water nymph or a mermaid. She must be something else.

He brought her to a steakhouse for their next date. He stuffed his mouth with meat and watched her push her salad around her plate.

"Not much of a carnivore?" he asked her.

Serena smiled at him quizzically. "That's a rather unusual question, Andros."

He swallowed and then grinned, his teeth sharp in the dim lighting. "I don't mean it to be. I love a good steak. I could eat one every night. But you ordered a salad. Does meat make you feel... unclean?"

Her laughter wasn't mean at all, and Andros mentally checked off his list. She wasn't a werewolf. She wasn't a golden dragon or a vampire. She didn't seem at all menacing, so nothing predatory. He tried one more question.

"Do you ever feel like life is eternal? That you've lived eons already and have a couple thousand more to go?"

She sighed. "I do feel that way sometimes. I get very weary."

It really wasn't a very good question. Immortality applied to most of the Otherkind. Still, he had asked and she had answered, and that was a very good thing, indeed.

That night Andros had a dream. He and Serena were walking

through the forest. She was a daughter of the moon, stars shining in her dark hair and eyes. She wore a long white dress and her hand was resting on the ruff of Andros's neck.

Andros realized he was padding by her side on all fours. He glanced down and saw soft brown paws. He twitched his ears and slashed his tail through the air. He sniffed and could smell the anticipation emanating from Serena's pores.

She stopped suddenly, knelt down and rubbed her face into Andros's fur. "It's nearly time, my love," she murmured. Andros whimpered and licked her ear, leaving red stains on her white skin. Blood. His mouth was full of it and it invigorated him. He raised his muzzle to the moon and howled.

The next day he was unusually quiet. Serena slipped her cold fingers into his.

"Are you all right?" she asked him.

He bit his lip, tasted blood, and thought of his dream. He found it exciting.

"Serena, do you ever feel that…we're more than we seem? That we could peel our skins away and find something wild and animalistic underneath?"

Her eyes told him everything he needed to know.

"That's a very deep thought," she said. "You're treading on dangerous territory." She was teasing, but he could feel the truth was threading through her words. Of course it was. This wasn't something that she could speak about openly. If she did, the enchantment would be broken, and she would have to go back to wherever she came from. That's why she chose to speak to Andros in dreams. That's why she chose to let him in on the secret that he was an Other, too. Moon and Wolf. *Luna e Volk.* Perhaps he never would have figured it out on his own. The thought made him shudder.

He had to let her know that he understood. That he was ready.

"It's a full moon tonight," he said casually. Serena's face softened.

"I know. I've been looking forward to it."

Of course she had. "Would you like to do something special?" Her eyes glowed.

Andros picked her up after dark. It was a long drive out of the city and to the forest, but it would be worth it. At first he was disappointed Serena was wearing a dark dress instead of the white one from the dream, but it made her creamy skin even more luminous in comparison. Besides, she wouldn't be wearing it for too much longer, anyway.

"I'm very glad to be here with you," she said, and dropped her hand lightly on Andros's thigh. "I think that tonight will be very memorable."

He couldn't drive there fast enough. Finally he found the clearing, a place that he remembered from years ago. He parked the car, got out, and opened the door for Serena. She stepped lightly out of the car and turned her face to the moon.

"It's so beautiful."

It was. So was she. Andros was shocked to find the feeling he felt was...gratitude. He was grateful that she was going to show him her true self. He was grateful that he'd get to discover his.

"So how do we go about this?" he asked her. In the movies that he watched, the changes occurred without a man being aware of it. One minute he was walking along and the next he was growing bigger, larger, stronger. So now that Andros knew he was a wolf, how would it be different?

Serena's smile held mysteries. "Are you nervous?"

"A little," he said honestly.

She stepped closer and pulled his arms around her. "Don't be. It's a natural thing. You'll know exactly what to do."

Her kiss tasted like the sky. She stepped back and let her dress fall to the ground. Her body shone in the moonlight and Andros knew exactly who she was.

"Tennyo," he whispered.

"Hmm?"

She was a daughter of the moon, a daughter of the sky. She flew on feathered wings. There were tales about her kind in all of the old stories. The beautiful girl who turns into a swan. The woman who falls from the sky until her clothes are stolen from her. But there was more than that, wasn't there? It ran deeper. It was under her skin, under the flesh.

"You drink the stars," he murmured.

"You say pretty things."

He couldn't stop himself. "How is it going to be? Will I feel my skin tear? Will it hurt? Is it just this amazing feeling of coming together, of being who I really am?" He looked at her intensely. "Will you still care for me afterward? Will you be frightened?"

She pulled off his shirt, ran her open mouth down his throat. "Andros, you're so funny. Why would I be frightened?" She pressed closer.

"Maybe I'll be a monster. You'll be beautiful and I'll be hideous. Maybe I won't be able to control myself and I'll hurt you."

"You worry too much, darling."

It was time. He slid his hands down her smooth, bare back. Her skin reflected the moon's light like a star. He was dying to find out what was underneath it. He wanted to see—

"—who you truly are," he said.

"What?" she asked, and then she was screaming.

The knife was out of his back pocket and sliding down that beautiful spine of hers. It cut through easily, creating a seam in her suit of skin. She pulled away but he was stronger.

"I'm almost through, Serena. Your beauty is legendary. If you look like this in your human form, than how..."

He didn't finish. Serena was screaming, kicking and struggling. He knocked her down to the ground and pinned her with his long legs.

"Why are you fighting? I don't understand!"

She was saying things that didn't make sense. Andros thought maybe she was asking him why. He thought she was cursing him and begging for her father. He started cutting down the front, working the smooth, starry skin off in patches.

"Why don't you make this easier?" he asked her. He was starting to panic. Why was there so much blood? Why didn't her body slip off like silk and show him the wonders underneath? This never happened in the movies! Sometimes the skin needed a gentle tug from a loving suitor's hand, but never more than that.

"I can't be wrong. You showed all the signs!" He shook her, but she wasn't responding anymore. She was still breathing, but her eyes had gone someplace far away, farther away than the stars from which she...from which he *thought* she had come.

He looked at his hands. He looked at her body. She was red and raw, missing a breast. Blood and other fluids leaked from under her skin. He wanted to piece her back together, but the idea of pulling and tugging her shredded flesh into place made him sick. He turned his head to the side and vomited.

"Serena?" he whispered. There was no movement except for her shallow breathing. He called her name again and nervously wiped his mouth with the back of a dripping hand. He tasted something tangy and nearly familiar, and then realized that it was her blood. Serena's blood, smeared over his face and onto his lips. It was just like his dream, but twisted and brutally ugly. Where was the joy? Where was the rapture?

The knife glimmered as it fell from his shaking hand. Andros raised his face to the moon and screamed. In the shattered darkness, it sounded very much like the howling of an animal.

STARS

The Universe had it in for Samson Gimble. It was rollicking along doing Great Big Universy Things, when suddenly It realized that Great Big Universy Things are fine for the most part, but It wanted something more, something exciting and wonderful. Black holes and nebulas are intricate, and the Universe was adept at putting them together, but they were old hat. What was something that the Universe had never done before?

Ah, yes. Murder.

There was nothing about Sam that you would find especially notable. He was a generally goodhearted man, dressing rather quietly and performing his civic duty. He bites his ice cream instead of licking it, has three dogs all named Oliver, and never yells at children. That's Sam.

The Universe picked Sam at random, basically closing Its eyes and throwing a metaphysical dart into the world—*PING!* Farewell, Samson Gimble. The Universe chuckled and rubbed Its colossal hands together gleefully. Feeling unexpectedly perky, It began working on Its Rube Goldberg machine to bring about Sam's tragic and delightful death. What fun!

Now it seems rather unfair that on one hand we have Sam, and on the other is the Infinite Universe itself. "What a terrible story!" you could say, and you would be quite right. But take heart, for this is a story full of wonder and fancy, and in such stories, magical things often happen.

However, occasionally there is a person on this earth who is shivering outside on their back porch, looking upward for pleasure or for answers. There is usually something about them, a sense of need that shines out of their eyes and flashes up into the sky, for example, or just a general glitter that catches the star's attention. Stars like glitter. A star would have no problem plucking itself out of the sky and flitting down to Earth if it thinks that you are shiny enough to entertain it.

Sam was shiny enough to entertain the most curious star. He was positively pulsing with light, a country boy recently moved to the big city. He couldn't even see the stars at night for the bright neon lights, but that didn't mean that he didn't cut through the smog sharply himself. He was beautiful.

A tiny star, fairly new, watched the glittering light of Sam bobble through the rainy night, and with a cry of joy wrenched itself out of the fabric of sky and spiraled down to meet its new plaything.

Sam sat on a warped park bench located in a tiny sliver of green in the middle of the city. It was the closest thing to the country that he could find in this filthy town, and even then it was a far cry from the hills back at home. He had tried cursing for a while, but it didn't do any good, so now he did the next best thing.

He drank.

So, naturally, when the star came spiraling down out of the sky and landed on the grass, Sam didn't give it much thought.

"Nice," he said, and threw his bottle at it.

The star pulsed a little bit and then glided closer to Sam's shoes. It peered at his shoelace.

"Bug off," he said.

The star didn't bug off. It chimed brightly and hopped onto Sam's instep, inspecting the cheap leather.

"I hate stars."

The star believed this wasn't true.

"It *is* true! I really, really hate stars," Sam insisted.

The star shimmied up the leg of Sam's pants and nestled into his lap. It bobbed around for a bit and looked around in wonder.

"Quit trying to be cute. It's not going to work," Sam warned.

The star glowed furiously and began to purr. It was very pleased with its bright, shiny new plaything. Sam put his hand over it gently. It pressed into his palm and purred harder.

"Oh, all right. You win."

The star smiled and twinkled happily. They were going to have lots and lots of fun together, it and its new toy.

The Universe watched this new development in consternation. It very much hoped this little star didn't stay around for long. It was still hard at work on Its plans.

From then on, Sam never went anywhere without his star. He slid it into his shirt pocket and wandered out into the street, careful to keep an ear out to hear what it had to say.

It often had quite a bit to say. It chimed and whistled and shook stardust in its excitement to see everything that went on around it. It often peeped out of Sam's pocket, a tiny glowing fragment of light, and Sam had to gently push it back inside.

"Sorry, buddy, you can't just leap out here. Wait until we're somewhere that you won't be seen."

The star would wait patiently in the bottom of the pocket until suddenly it was overcome by its curiosity again. It would twinkle and glow, taking in every new scene and keeping a wary eye on that devious devil, the Universe. The tiny star had grown quite attached to its Sam, and was loath to lose him.

"Hey, I told you to keep out of sight," Sam whispered, and shook his head. "I don't know what I'm going to do with you."

The star slid obediently down into the pocket, but not before it shook its tiny fist at the sky. You've got something to contend with, Universe. Oh yes.

Today was the day that Sam was going to die. The star simply wasn't having it.

"Leave me alone," Sam mumbled into his pillow early on Saturday. The star chimed insistently in his ear, leaving burning little pinpricks on the lobe where it jumped around.

"Leave." Sam flipped over and pulled the pillow over his head, but the star managed to burrow under it and glow sternly. Sam swatted it away. The star bristled. Growling a little, it marched up to Sam's nose, touched it with a quivering point and promptly scorched it.

"What the—?" Sam yelled and flung the covers back, clasping both hands to his nose. He glared at the star with watery eyes. "Why would you do something like that?" The star meandered calmly away, and Sam, cursing, pulled on his jeans and started after it.

"No, you are not walking away from me. We are going to

142

discuss this behavior." Sam stopped in the middle of his kitchen. "I'm arguing with a star. With a *star*." He sank into the kitchen chair and rubbed his eyes. "I'm going crazy."

The star hissed at him, and then nudged a bottle of vitamins his way. Sam looked at them, and then at the star. "What are you, my wife?" The star was unmoved. Sam sighed and palmed the vitamins. This was going to be a long day.

If only he knew.

Today the Universe had something fun and whimsical up Its sleeve. It was quite cheery about the death of Samson Gimble. It hummed a little as It went to work. It was this happy, off-key rumbling that set the star on edge.

During breakfast, Sam took out a sharp, lethal-looking knife to peel his Granny Smith apple in one long peel. "EEP!" squeaked the star, and flung itself across the room, smacking into Sam's hand and forcing him to drop the knife. It clattered to the floor.

"What is *with* you today?" he said, and reached down to pick the knife back up. The star guarded it fiercely. Sam finally stepped away.

"All right, all right, I get it. No knife, okay?" He held his hands up in surrender, and the star drooped in relief. Sam turned on the stove.

"ACK!" yelped the star, and flurried over to the stove, bouncing around in agitation until Sam hurriedly turned the burner off.

"Okay!" Sam said through gritted teeth. "No knives. No stove. Nothing delicious or homemade for me this morning."

Breakfast was that same Granny Smith apple, unpeeled. Sam munched it resentfully. The star preened.

About this time, on the other side of the world, the Universe was giggling. It was a lovely day in Japan, and the spring flowers were out. Particularly the Ayame, an exquisitely vibrant purple flower with long tongue-like petals that drape delicately from its stamen. The Universe had spent quite a long time on its creation, and it was quite proud. A young couple and their lovely baby (who, thanks to the Universe's not-so-innocent meddling, happened to be allergic to the Ayame flower) were admiring a particularly beautiful cluster when the baby sneezed.

"Bless you!" his mother said immediately, and reached in her purse for a tissue. This sudden movement startled a resting Appias albino butterfly, which is a particularly ethereal-looking butterfly with large white wings. It is not native to Japan, and had most likely been introduced to the area by a typhoon or whatnot (another of the Universe's delights), but here it was, and here it had planned to stay, resting by the Ayame flower. But, alas, that was not meant to be, and it fluttered its wings rather desperately. As we all learned in the third grade, a butterfly fluttering its wings in Japan can affect the weather system in the United States, and it really was a glorious lesson on how we are all intertwined on the great big beautiful planet that is Earth. What a warm and fuzzy demonstration indeed, except that warm fuzzies was not what the Universe had intended. It had just set into play the chain of events that would eventually kill Samson Gimble. The Universe grinned. So cliché, yet so delightful. It settled back to watch.

Back home, Sam was heading toward the door, much to the star's dismay. It buzzed and glowered and teetered as threateningly as it knew how, but Sam was determined to go along with his day as usual. After a brief chase, he managed to slip the star into his pocket and start out the door. The clouds were dark and heavy, but he thought little of it, even when the wind started to pick up. The star shivered.

"Hey, it's okay," Sam whispered to the star. His earlier anger had diminished, and now he was concerned for the star's distress. "You want me to tell you a story? Would that cheer you up?"

The star huddled in misery, and Sam began talking, oblivious to the looks that he was receiving on the street. He told the star about his family, where he grew up, about the family dog whose name changed weekly. This most likely explains why he chose to name all of his dogs Oliver now, but this is neither the time nor the place to psychoanalyze our Samson Gimble. We will surely get to that later.

If there is anything left to analyze, that is.

The star ceased trembling and listened, engrossed in the story but mostly in the glittering light that Sam gave off while telling it. Sam paused long enough to grab a few things at the grocery store, but then continued on again as soon as he was outside.

A flash of lightning interrupted him.

"This is crazy weather," he told the star. "Even for here."

The star narrowed its eyes and poked out of the pocket. Rain started to pour.

"Aw, man," Sam said, and picked up his pace.

The wind screamed and tore at the city. The star held onto Sam's pocket tightly, but still felt like it would be carried away. It looked around wildly for signs of danger.

A few buildings in front of them, a large pile of bricks had been left in a rather haphazard fashion on top of the roof. The wind pushed against the unsteady pile until one of the top bricks, already teetering, simply cried out its fond farewells and leapt from the roof.

The star noticed this, and with a tiny shriek it hurled itself out of its warm pocket and under Sam's feet. Sam's size 13 boot landed on it with a crunch that made even the Universe wince.

Sam gasped and stopped. He quickly knelt down to pick up the crushed star, and the brick whizzed less than six inches away from his head. He didn't notice.

Sam cradled the dimming star in his hands. The star blinked blearily at the shattered brick and his beautifully *unshattered* Sam, and let itself collapse. It basked in Sam's light and purred brokenly.

Sam placed it carefully into his shirt pocket. "Let's get you home, okay? I'll even let you sleep on the pillow." Deep in his heart, he knew there would be no more pillows for his little star, but he couldn't bear to think of it. He hoisted his grocery bags, careful not to jar his friend. He stepped neatly over the broken brick and hurried home.

The Universe was confused. All of Its hard work and scheming, and murder wasn't very fun at all. In fact, it was downright dismal. The Universe shifted uncomfortably when the faint glimmer in Sam's pocket went out. It was such a little star; surely it couldn't create much light. So why did everything seem so much darker than it did just moments before?

Samson Gimble dashed at his eyes. The Universe watched this silently before turning Its interest back to Life.

WINGS

Every time he sits down, his wings catch underneath him. They smack into the doorframe when he walks, pegs his sister in the eye if she isn't paying attention. He is always asked to play the dove or the pigeon or the heavenly angel in the community plays. Every time, he forgets his lines. Every time, he promises to do better.

At school he is knocked down, held to the ground while the bullies rip out his feathers. He tells his parents that it's the change in seasons and he is molting. Nobody mentions his black eyes and split lip. Molting can be hard on a young man.

One day in the cafeteria, a girl calls to him.

"Hey, you," she says. Never have those two words sounded so lovely, so uncommon.

"Boy," she says, and it is even more exquisite. He slowly turns to the girl.

She is beautiful, with eyes that never seem to blink. He stands, wings beating almost frantically, before walking over to her with his lunch tray.

"Please sit," she says, and points at the seat across from her. Her friends laugh, but she doesn't seem to notice them. He sits gingerly, ready to spring up before they dump his lunch tray on his chest—or whatever it is that they're going to do. His wings bump into the girls on either side of him. They squirm away.

The girl watches him with her pale eyes. He's nervous and his feathers ruffle.

She speaks. Her voice is like water. "I hear that you're quite good in chemistry, and I'm struggling. I was wondering...would you mind partnering up?"

Her friends gasp. Her eyes don't leave his. He's waiting for her to break face. He's waiting for the punch line.

She tilts her head to one side.

He swallows. "Uh...sure."

He's certain alarms will sound and confetti will fall into his lap. He's sure cameras will appear out of nowhere and tell him that he's on TV.

Instead, she smiles. Her teeth are like pearls. "I'm so glad," she says. His heart flips a bit. He wonders if this is what it's like to be in love.

She chooses a seat next to him in class. They bend over the book with their heads together. He explains why the experiment she proposes would explode and kill them all. He tells her how fireworks are made, what gives them the colors. She asks if she can come over and study the next evening. His wings flutter and he stutters out a yes.

His parents are thrilled. His mother drags him to the store to buy a new "studying shirt". She hums as she cuts out holes for his wings. His father shakes his head, but he's smiling.

When she comes over, she's wearing a white dress with her hair down, and she looks like a little girl. She clutches a stack of books to her chest and smiles at his father. She laughs with his mother and crosses her eyes at his sister. He comes quietly down the stairs and stands for a long time, looking at her. She hurts his eyes.

She comes over often to study. Her chemistry grade gets better, but still she comes. They go for walks. He lets her run her hand down the length of his wings, feeling the bones. She's surprised at the warmth of them. She bites her lip and then takes a deep breath. She will be dancing on stage soon, and...would he and his family like to come?

They go. She is lovely, and he can't stop watching. He walks her home and gives her a flower that has flattened in his sweaty fist. She tucks it into her hair, and it is exactly right.

They stand on the porch under the light. He wants to kiss her but is too nervous. She slips her chilly hand tentatively into his, and he calms. She shivers and he wraps his wings around both of them. They fit wonderfully, and she laughs.

She murmurs something. He wonders if he hears the word *love*.

He kisses her hair, his lips touching the flower that he gave her. She asks him to explain the difference between incandescence and luminescence, even though she already knows. She says she likes the way he uses his hands as he talks, the way that he tries not to gesture with his wings, which is fine because he'd rather keep them folded where they are.

She has an idea for chemistry; maybe it can be their project. She likes the way his lips turn up as he explains again that the laws of physics are like love in a way: they're beautiful and amazing and most importantly, unchanging...and, unfortunately, the experiment will still explode and kill them all.

"Unchanging?" she asks.

"Unchanging," he agrees. He gently touches his fingertips to her cheek. She takes his hand and touches his fingers to her lips, and then his own cheek.

Her eyes, they're like stars. His, they're full of hope. His wings barely even flutter.

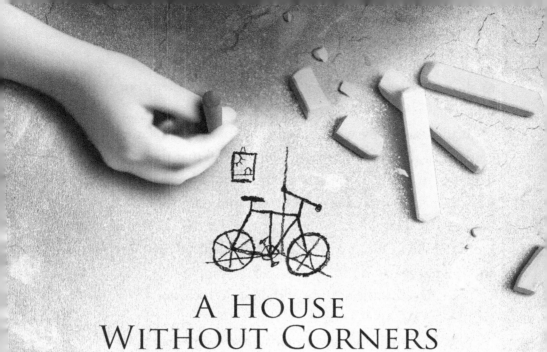

A HOUSE
WITHOUT CORNERS

It didn't take me very long to realize they were broken, two sisters who hadn't seen each other since they were little kids. They were just trying this out, getting to know each other again, they said. Would I like to move in? I was currently sharing a dorm room with several foreign exchange students. They stayed up all night and ate my food. They used my dishes and broke my plates. Of course, I wanted to move in with the sisters! They intrigued me. I found them delightful and charming.

They swung. They swung like I had never seen, depression to mania and back again. They booby trapped the toothpaste to see if I was using it. (I was.) They booby trapped the Ouija board to see if I was using that. (I wasn't.) They hung a picture of Jesus on the wall and said His eyes followed them around. Jesus shook every time a train went by.

Their parents, it turns out, were freaks in every sense of the word. If something was broken, their dad laid his hands on their heads and called out for the Holy Spirit to tell him who to punish. He tried to shout devils out of them. He tried to beat them out while their mother watched.

If they said they were hungry, he made them eat entire bags of chips until their tiny stomachs were so full that they vomited. He'd make them stand in corners for hours and hours. Then the sisters were ripped apart and sent to live in different homes. One of them bounced all around the country for years; the other had a little bit more stability. One day in college they magically ran into each other and invited me along.

"We have brothers," one of them told me once.

"Yeah? Where?" I asked.

She shrugged, and never mentioned them again.

Our house was owned by a family of illegal immigrants. It was a basement with several hidden exits in case the police came. Our cable was spliced from the main house, but we didn't know that. Our landlords charged us $65 dollars a month and came into our rooms without permission. We discovered a few pairs of our panties were missing and blamed each other at first. Gradually we stopped coming home. I slept in the loft of the newspaper building most nights. I spent a lot of my time there, anyway.

The house always smelled of cabbage because that's all my roommates would eat. They thought they were fat. They had a phobia of being full because of their father forcing them to vomit, so they constantly sipped at small portions of cabbage soup. They'd make elaborate meals and then ask my boyfriend and I eat to them.

"Eat more," they'd say. "Eat more."

It made me uncomfortable, but I'd do it, their eyes upon me hungrily. Then they'd take another spoonful of cabbage soup.

Our house was a house without corners. Every angle had

something rounded shoved there, like a houseplant or a bicycle. They couldn't be forced to stand in a corner that didn't exist.

"Your father doesn't live here," I boldly said one night. They didn't speak to me for weeks.

They had pet rats, and the rats had babies. Then the babies had babies. The house had no bedroom doors, but it did have secret passages. I could walk through my closet and end up in their room. I heard them mimicking me at night. They held my cat down and cut off her whiskers with scissors. It was a house of open wounds. It was a house of hate.

We all drove the same car in different colors, parking them in the driveway side by side by side. If you didn't know any better, you'd look at those cheery matching cars and think, "They must be friends." It might make you smile.

When I moved out, they filled my bag with rotted vegetables and the contents from the vacuum bag. I shook ash and dust out of my journal. Cat hair. More whiskers.

It was a house of secrets. A house of lies. I learned how to exorcise it myself.

SWEET, SWEET SONJA T

His eyes had caught on her name many times. *Sonja*. They scanned smoothly over the rest of the page, but something about the ripe, ready to burst "S" of her name made his eyes give pause. Sonja T. Lansom. What was the "T" for? Tammy? Tabatha? The stories that she submitted to his magazine were sweet. Simple. Charming, for the most part, but he wanted something a little more visceral.

"I feel that you are holding back," he commented once. A personalized rejection letter, not something that he did often, but he wanted to for her. "Don't hold back anymore. I'd love you to send something else to me, Sonja. Strip down your façade. Peel away your layers. Show me who you really are."

It took two more stories, hesitantly written. He politely rejected them as well, but continued to encourage her. Like a young girl approaching womanhood, she was changing. He could smell it, see it in the way that her vocabulary unfolded its wings like locusts. So discreet. So maidenly. So afraid, when all he wanted was for her to trust him, so that he could get to know her, really know her.

"Try again, Sonja. Try again."

Then one day, she sent it. The story. The one that he always knew was inside of her. He read it, groaned, read it again. He left the computer, walked outside, leaned against the gatepost. Went back inside, sat back down. Read it again. And again.

Then he called her.

Sweet Sonja. So trusting with her information, if not her writing. Her name, her address. Her phone number typed neatly at the top of the manuscript. He picked up the phone and discovered that his hand was unusually clammy. He wiped it off on his jeans, dialed the number carefully, and held the phone too close to his mouth.

It rang. It rang.

"Hello?"

Her voice was lovely. He knew it was hers right away. The sound of music playing in the background, something old. Something from the 40s.

"Sonja," he said, and it thrilled him.

"Hold on a second, would you? Let me turn the music down."

The sound in the background was suddenly much quieter.

"That's better," she said, and he was struck silent by the laughter that seemed to run under her words. What would she be laughing at? What wonderful things would she see, there by the seashore? He looked at her address even though he knew it by heart—1871 Benson, small town by the coast. Did she hear gulls? Were the woody trees scented with brine?

"Hello?" she said again, and when he didn't answer, she simply hung up.

The sound—*click*—made his shoulders draw in. *Click*. How impersonal. How absolutely final.

But then, she didn't have any idea that it was him. It could be anyone, any old crazy from the street calling her number. She'd want to protect herself, savvy girl. Savvy woman. His Sonja, his bright prodigy.

He called his boss. "It's time that we go on tour," he said. "I want to do some speaking engagements. Put a little money in our pockets, promote the mag. There's a college by the sea. Charming little place. How about I do it there?"

The e-mail was a masterpiece. Polite without being stuffy, formal enough to be professional but with a casual, lackadaisical flair.

My dear Sonja,

I will soon be coming to your area to speak at a conference. Would you be at all interested in attending? I would like to discuss your latest story with you. It is fantastic, both vicious and tenderly written. A gloriously beautiful tragedy and we would be most pleased to publish it.

Come see me after the conference if you can attend, and if not, we will most certainly hammer out the details through email.

All the best,
JB, Editor

Her reply was instant. "Oh yes, I would love to attend! Thank you so much for accepting my story! You have certainly made my day."

He got a haircut, he started jogging. Time would soon come when he would meet his divine Sonja T. Lansom.

She was heartbreakingly lovely. He had looked her up online, of course, found a few pictures. A blog written by her sister-in-law, who had four children and a penchant for polar bears. It was tedious reading for the most part, but a brief "and then S. came over for dinner" made his heart twitch. There was a picture of Sonja holding one of the kids, her face turned to the side and laughing. No signs of a husband. Sonja had also started an Author's page, and had a black and white picture at the head. Sweet girl, eyes a bit too large, but time and hard experience would take care of that. Her hair was carefully combed down in the picture, pulled into a ponytail that fell over one shoulder. She was wearing a soft white sweater that endeared her to him even more. A full mouth that practically trembled in the photo. So unsure of herself, so young. He'd take out anybody that ever hurt her, he decided. Right then and there. They would deserve it.

Whoa, he thought suddenly. Going back to my youth. I thought I'd stamped out that part of me long ago. My sweet, sweet Sonja T, look what you've done.

He lectured, he spoke, he bantered wittily during the Q&A. She didn't raise her hand, which was a shame, but she watched everything with her lips slightly parted, her eyes sparkling. Luminous. Gray moons. Her hair wasn't as sleek as her picture, and he liked that. It railed against the barrette that tried to tie it down. It sought him out. It waved in the air like a living thing, tentacles reaching for his words. He imagined that his breath moved it, made it sway from side to side like underwater weeds. She ducked her head from time to time and her hair fell in front of her eyes. Shielding her. Hiding, from his intensity, the bright, burning light that was him. Engaging girl.

Afterward, she tentatively crept up to him. Slim black pants, a purple top cinched at her waist with a belt, tiny ballet flats. The shoes charmed him, an Audrey Hepburn in a nearly steampunk world.

Her lipstick had been eaten away long ago, and she smiled at him timidly.

"Hello," she said, and stopped. She caught her breath, started again. "Hello," she said, and held out her hand. Her fingers were warm and soft. He held the handshake exactly four seconds longer than normal—he counted in his head—and reluctantly dropped her trembling fingers. She slid her hands into her sleeves, clutched girlishly at the cuffs, pale fingers peeping out. Baby birds.

"Hello," he said back, and smiled wide. This gave her new courage.

"Hello, I'm...I'm Sonja T. Lansom. I...you said that you were going to publish my story." She wavered on her feet a little, and he gallantly took her arm, helped her sit down. She tucked her feet under her chair.

"Yes, Sonja. Let us discuss your wonderful story. Would you like to do it now? Actually, I'm quite hungry. Would you possibly have time to come with me while I grab a bite to eat? We could discuss it there? Or if you would rather..."

"Oh, no," she said quickly, and touched his hand briefly with her delicate fingers. Just a second (less than that, really), but his body roared hot at the touch. "Certainly, let's get you something to eat. I know a café around the corner, if that sounds at all like something... something that you..."

She floundered, the reticent thing. Sweet, sweet Sonja T.

"That sounds great," he said, and offered her his arm.

They chose a table on the patio. He ordered meatloaf and mashed potatoes with pie. She had a salad with pecans and mandarin oranges. No wonder she's so tiny. So light. He held his breath every now and then so as not to blow her out to sea.

"Your story, it was so raw," he said, leaning forward. She leaned forward, too. Into him. Attracted by his pull, drawn into his source of gravity. It made him smile, and she shyly smiled back.

"I'm so happy that you liked it," she whispered, and he reached out for her bare hands on the table. She frowned briefly but then it was gone. He'd have to be careful not to scare her, or else she'd rabbit out of there. He pulled his hands away until their fingers were barely touching.

"I do like it. We, everybody at the magazine, simply loved it. I felt like you really broke through, Sonja." Sonja, Sonja, Sonja. "It was like there was a wall that you scaled. No, you didn't scale it; you completely kicked it down. However did you kick down your wall, Sonja? Tell me. I am simply dying to know."

She chewed her bottom lip. He raised his eyebrows, made his eyes sparkle. Ta-*DING!* He was interested, friendly. Worthy of her trust. She was lost, needed to confide. Talk to me, my girl.

"You really want to know?" she asked. Her gray eyes were doubtful. Sweet Sonja T, she didn't trust herself yet. She didn't trust *him.* She would, in time. He covered her hands with his again. She didn't move them away, instead nestled her fingers inside. He shielded her hands, protecting them. Like a mother bird, like a layer of ozone. Shielding, warming, guiding. A bomb shelter before a nuclear holocaust.

"Of course I want to know," he said, and pressed his hands more tightly to hers. "Tell me, Sonja T."

She hitched a breath. "I...made a choice one day. To do something that I have always wondered about. To do something that I have always wanted to do, but was too afraid. I decided that I didn't want to be that kind of person anymore." She looked up, trying to read him. "Do you understand?"

He nodded wisely. Sagely. "I do," he said kindly. "I do. Go on."

She swallowed. "Finally one day I had enough. I said, You know what? I spend all of my life being afraid. That somebody will find me. That somebody will hurt me. I follow all of the rules, do everything that I'm supposed to do. I have never...I have never..."

She loves me, he thought. Just look at her. Here holding my hands, telling me secrets at a quaint little café. The ocean breeze blowing her hair off of her face. He shivered just a bit, and her fingers tucked into her fists in response. Poor little birds, always hiding. He thought of her house, of the way the lights flicked on and off as she walked from room to room. He wondered what her routine would be before going to bed, how long it would take until he was part of her routine as well. Toothbrushes side by side, smiling a little as she straightened his razor. Poor Editor JB, he's such a slob. Good thing she's there to take care of him. How did he ever get by without her?

"So what is your scandalous secret, Sonja? You can tell me." He was dying. *He was dying.*

She smiled. It was lovely, wide as the sea. Her eyes were dreamy. "My secret? Is that I'm not afraid anymore. I am strong. Stronger than he thought."

His soul crushed. His heart broke. His hands melted like something painted by Dali.

"He?" he asked.

"What?" she said. Her eyes were huge. "What he?"

"Your he. Your 'you're stronger than he thought' he."

She looked panicked. "You misheard! There is no he. At least, not anymore." Her moonlight eyes caught his. Trapped him. He read them, was still reading when her lashes fluttered down over them.

Her story. Her dark, brutal, visceral story.

"Ah," he said.

Her face was white. Oleander white, except for a flush high on both cheeks. She started to pull her hands away.

"My sweet, sweet Sonja T," he said.

She paused, didn't look at him. Needing a sign. Needing acceptance.

He sighed, leaned back in his chair, threaded his fingers through hers. "What say you and I run off to Finland?" he offered casually.

"F-Finland?"

"Yes."

She thought about it. "How do they say 'hello' in Finland?"

"*Hei*," he responded. *Hei. Hei, Sonja.*

Her smile broke something inside of him. Sternum tearing off and puncturing his heart. Heimlich given by a 400-pound gorilla. It felt good.

"I could do that," she said.

BLOSSOM BONES

She was beautiful before she died; but afterward? Ah, she was exquisite. He couldn't look at her enough, couldn't touch her fingers enough. She was all hair and gentle silence and, after a while, ribbons of bones.

He carried her everywhere, dressed in delicate dresses with a pink parasol tied to her hand. He told her stories about his childhood. He sang sweet lullabies. He set her in her favorite spot, the garden, and the vines twisted around her femurs and made love to her ribs. She was coolness and full of night blooming flowers. Her eyes shone Delphiniums.

EDIBILITY

"**T**ink electrocuted himself today. No joke. Remember the bobcat thrown over the power lines? Just like that. Tink climbed up there to see if things looked any different."

She was sitting in the flowers, eating petals. She examined each one individually before gently placing it on her tongue, closing her mouth and savoring.

"So the funeral is Thursday. The bobcat, right? Remember how it fell to the ground and started on fire? Man, I never thought I'd see anything like that again! And now Tink. It was just awesome."

They had a lawn once, but she had pulled it all out, first by hand and then with a shovel. She had lain in the black dirt, sucking at the grass roots in search of nectar she never found. Then she had pulled seeds out of her pockets, all manner of seeds. No grass now, only flowers.

"The guys are going out to shoot pool tonight, wanted to know if I'd come. I said you wouldn't mind. You don't mind, do you, baby? I thought not. I'll bring something home when I come. Something with pecans for the morning. I'll make it good."

She was baking lemon cakes today, but he didn't notice or didn't care, and this did not bother her. She stood up, carefully picking her way through the flowers, a bunch of purple and yellow johnny-jump-ups in her hand. He tromped over the flowers, crushing blooms as he went, but it was all right. She could get them to raise their heads again.

"So, later, darlin'. Don't stay up too late. I'll get back when I get back."

He pressed a kiss into her hair, and she smiled at him. The flowers screamed as he headed to the car, but she gave them a little wink, and they calmed.

The lemon cakes were shaped like stars. They cooled on the windowsill because this house was their own little suburbia, and such things were allowed. She removed the heads of the johnnys and floated them in a bowl of chilled water.

She mixed together powdered sugar and milk, added vanilla and frosted the cakes. She carefully laid the johnnys side by side on a clean dish towel to dry.

The cat wrapped around her leg. She sent it outside to chase the flowers, who squealed merrily when the cat batted at their petals. The cat hummed.

Once dry, she sprinkled the johnnys on the star cakes. The cakes were beautiful, cheery little things, and she waited for somebody to come by and ask for one. Somebody always did.

Two goldfish swam in a bowl resting in the hollowed out TV. "Shhh," she whispered to the bigger one, who was complaining. She crumpled up a little bit of cake in her hands, let it fall into the water like sand. The johnny-jump-ups swirled across the top of the water to their own music.

She curled up in the chair, slipped a blanket over her translucent body. She opened a book but didn't read, instead running her hand across the words on the paper. If she took scissors, cut the paper into the shape of a mask and peered through, what would she see? What would she see?

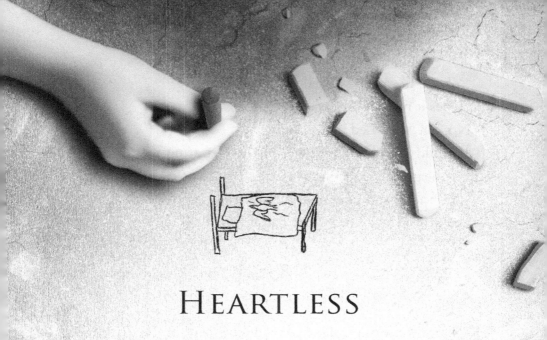

HEARTLESS

"It's snowing outside and I would like to sleep in your bed, please."

The voice was unfamiliar and she turned over to see who was speaking.

"I'd appreciate it if you wouldn't look at me."

He sounded so reasonably polite and yet so cold that she quickly resumed her hunched position.

"Who are you?" she asked. She was strangely calm. She felt pleased to feel any emotion at all.

"I only want to sleep. Nothing else." He slid under the covers on the empty side of the bed. There was no pillow there. She felt the heat radiate from his skin, and was vaguely grateful for it. She had caught a chill two Christmases ago and it had never gone away.

She should leap from the bed and run screaming for the door. She should fight for her life if he chose to steal it. But was it worth fighting for? Her eyelids were already starting to droop. Unusual, considering that she generally stared at the shadowy walls until the early hours of morning.

"You're not going to tell me who you are?"

"Does it matter?" he asked.

No. She supposed that it didn't.

"Would you like a pillow?" She was starting to slur her words, and she heard the smile in his voice. It was not reassuring.

"I'm fine, thank you. You should really go to sleep."

She drifted away before he had finished talking.

The next morning she woke up refreshed for the first time since her husband's death. She sat up quickly and looked at the other side of the bed, but it was empty. The blankets had been disturbed, although whether by her nightmares or a visitor, she couldn't tell.

"Odd," she said, and rummaged around in her dresser for her exercise gear. She hadn't gone running in months.

When she returned, she showered and went about her day until night relentlessly fell again. She read cookbooks and scrubbed bathtubs and did everything that she could think of to fill her time, but eventually she slid a soft nightshirt over her head, brushed her teeth, and climbed into bed. She turned on her side and stared at the wall. An hour passed.

She pulled her knees up to her chest, but still shivered.

"You always seem to be cold."

She started, but before she could turn toward the voice it said, "Remember that you are not to look at me, please."

"But why not?" she asked, carefully keeping her back to him. She felt him slide into the bed.

"It's personal."

"And this isn't?"

There was a pause before the voice said, "Would you rather that I leave?"

She thought about it for a while. It would be much wiser to ask him to go. But Christmas was coming, and she couldn't bear to be alone for it. And quite frankly, she didn't have much to lose.

"No, you can stay. But," she said evenly, "are you going to kill me?"

"Not at the moment, no. Although it wouldn't really upset either one of us if I did, now, would it?"

She didn't answer and knew he didn't expect her to. She counted her breaths—one, two, three—and then she was asleep.

The next night he brought her some holly. The night after that, he left her a dead bird. She became used to him and realized with mild surprise that the faint alarm bells going off were so quiet and listless that they were easy to ignore. It seemed almost normal, their brief minute of conversation and then sleep. She didn't even keep her back to him anymore, but merely closed her eyes when he entered so as to give him the privacy that he demanded. Sometimes she caught a faint coppery smell, but it was almost familiar and not too unpleasant, so she put it out of her mind. She put everything out of her mind. It wasn't at all difficult to do.

One night he said to her, "You miss your husband." It was simply stated, but not necessarily heartless.

She slid her hand into his, and didn't care when he didn't close his fingers around hers.

"We're all going to die," she said. Her voice was quiet and steady.

He took her hand, pulled it up to rest on his heart. She felt the heat from his skin, but no movement beneath his ribs.

"Yes," he said. He pulled her fingers to his mouth and kissed them, one by one. "Yes, you are."

"You sound sad," she said. She buried her face into his shoulder and sighed. She thought of her father, how he must smell in his grave now. She wondered if he felt the cold or saw the poinsettias that she left for him.

"I might be sad," he said. His voice sounded like the wind. She didn't notice the tears running down her face.

"What do you want from me?" she asked him softly. She remembered holding her best friend's wrists together in high school, the blood running over her hands. The warmth of it had been startling.

He was silent for a long time. He rubbed his chin against the side of her face. She stared at the ceiling, thinking of the moment that she had heard Eric had shot himself in junior high. His brother always fed Eric's kittens to their dogs.

"Do you think that you could love me?" he asked.

She knew worms crawled through her husband's eyes. They had been light green.

"The things that I think when I'm with you…" Birds pecking holes in her skin.

"I know," he said. "I think that I am sorry. It is the nature of things."

She held her breath. He smelled of death and all things abandoned. She couldn't hear him breathe.

"Would you want me to love you?" she asked him.

He didn't speak again. Not for several more nights.

She began showering every day. Brushing her hair. She pulled the worn box of holiday decorations out and slowly put them up. They glittered and it was almost beautiful.

"Blood," she said one evening. His hand wrapped around hers. "It's blood that I smell on you."

"Yes."

"I want to ask. But you wouldn't tell me, would you?"

"No."

"Then don't ask me to love you."

The next time that he came, her hair had grown two inches. She had stopped eating and had lost more pounds than her frame could afford. The holiday decorations adorned the walls and mantel, just in time for Christmas. She hadn't taken them down since he'd left her last year.

"I can't seem to sleep without you," she said. "Why would that be?"

He ran his fingers along her cheekbone, into the gaunt hollows underneath.

"I do not know," he said. "But you are unwell. That is why I am here."

She turned onto her back, stared at the ceiling.

"I hear carols in my head. That's supposed to be a good thing, yes?"

He didn't say anything. The warmth of his body slowly melted her chill.

She turned into his side, rested her head on his still chest. She grabbed his shirt with both hands.

"For a while, I thought that you were Kristopher coming back. That somehow..."

"I am not your husband."

"I know that now."

He ran his hand down her hair.

"I could...find him for you. If you wanted. He wouldn't be the same, but I could—"

"No."

He fell silent.

"I could love you," she said.

He grabbed her chin and forced her to look at his face. His eyes were hot blackness, but she reached out her hand and laid it on his cheek. Her skin felt like it was singeing. She nearly winced.

"I am of the darkness," he warned. "I can only bring horror." His teeth were sharp, but she couldn't blame him for that. It wasn't his doing.

"Horror is relative," she said, and smiled at him for the first time. When he smiled back, her heart only dropped a little.

PIXIES DON'T GET NAMES

I was buying a six-foot one-inch stuffed shark from FAO
Schwartz. A hammerhead. It was quite charming.

"I need it," I explained to the cashier as he struggled to find
its price tag.

"*Umph*," he answered me from somewhere under the shark's
belly. I couldn't be quite sure where.

"You know. To help me sleep. I have nightmares," I confided,
sliding my credit card and signing my name. The cashier handed the
shark to me gingerly. I could barely fit my arms around it.

"You have nightmares so you're getting a *shark*?" he asked me.
I peeked around from behind one of the hammerhead's wide eyes.

"Well, yeah. Sharks are tough and ferocious, right? Don't you
think they'd keep a good eye on nightmares?"

The cashier battled the urge to roll his eyes, I could tell. "And
what, pray tell, do you have nightmares about?"

"Pixies," I said, and the cashier threw his hands in the air helplessly.

"I don't think he believed you," the pixie sang from my shoulder.

"Most people don't," I said. Then, "I wish that you were bigger
and could help me carry this shark to the car."

"Me, too," the pixie said wistfully. He ran his tiny hand down the shark's fur. "It's a beautiful shark," he said graciously.

"Thank you. I think so, too."

Carrying the gigantic stuffed toy was no small feat. I dragged his tail on the floor and tripped over it. He got caught in the doorway twice, in the escalator once, and I nearly knocked a gangsta wannabe to the floor.

I heard him shout something about disrespect, and watched some baggy pants dancing around, but I couldn't see any more than that over the shark.

"Huh? What?" I spun around a couple of times, but when I failed to ever see the guy face to face, I just gave up and left.

"*Whew,*" I said, after stuffing the shark in the backseat of the car. "That was tougher than I thought it was going to be!" Of course it was. My car is a blue Geo Metro.

"I love you," chimed the pixie. He patted my cheek gently with his tiny hand.

"Well...thanks," I told him, and hopped into the driver's seat.

He flew from my shoulder to the top of the steering wheel. "No, I really, really love you. You don't act like you believe me."

I don't know if you've ever seen a pixie pout, but it's hilarious. Their pointy ears droop and their entire bodies sag like their bones have just dissolved. This particular pixie was practically oozing from my steering wheel in distress. I managed to keep the smile off of my face and I leaned in close to the suffering pixie.

"You know what?" I asked him. He tried to act uninterested, but he couldn't hide the shine in his eyes. "I believe you," I said, nodding to show my sincerity. "I do."

Instantly he straightened up and zipped into the air. "It's settled, then!" He shimmered his wings with joy. "Let us speak of our wedding!" The stuffed shark peered over the back seat with glassy eyes, but for the pixie, he was a fine audience. "First we shall have the most exquisite of foods," he informed the shark, "and then, dancing!"

I backed the car into reverse and maneuvered carefully onto the street. "Watch out," I warned the pixie, and then the little Geo shot onto the freeway. There was a tiny "woo-hoo!" and we were battling the traffic back home.

The thing about pixies is that they have an astronomically short life cycle. A day, actually. So this little pixie had been born at dawn, hit puberty by lunch and now that it was twilight, he was more than a little past his prime. In short, his biological clock was ticking like crazy, and he knew it.

"Your hair would look lovely in braids," he said, and grunted as I swerved out of the way of a drifting semi. He paused, his lovely green hair blowing in the breeze of my air conditioner. "Have you ever worn braids?"

"Yes, two days ago," I said, and his face lit up. "Two days ago! Was that the fashion back in those times?"

"Sure," I said, concentrating more on my driving than his words. I caught a glimpse of his wings drooping out of the corner of my eye. Quickly, I said, "So tell me more about what you'll be wearing?"

"Oh, it shall be glorious!" he began, and zipped around eagerly in the car. Even the shark looked bored.

"Dirk," I said aloud.

The pixie stopped in his tracks. "Beg pardon?"

"That's what I think I'll name the shark. Dirk. With...some sort of Russian last name, maybe. What do you think?"

The pixie eyed the shark. "Dirk the Hammerhead. With something Russian. Yes, it's perfectly lovely! He can attend our wedding!"

Pixies can't live without love, so they find it wherever they can. Usually that's me. It's seldom that two pixies will hatch out at my house on the same day, although it's happened twice. The first time, they were a lovely couple who asked me to be Godmother to their child. The other two were women who sat around writing mopey poetry about beautiful pixie-men.

"Why so sad?" I had asked one of them.

She had shaken her head in disbelief. "Imagine going *your* whole life without ever seeing a boy!"

She had me at that.

I was relieved to pull off the freeway, toward home. Once there, I grabbed Dirk-Something-Russian the Hammerhead out of the backseat and clumsily carted him up to the house.

"I'll always love you," the pixie said, eyes shining. "Until the end of time. Until absolutely forever. I'll never stop loving you, not until the end of my days."

I smiled at him. That last bit was partly true: he would love me until the end of his day. And that would only be about half an hour more. My smile faltered a little.

"Come on," I said to my jubilant pixie. "Let's go throw Dirk on the bed and see how he likes it there."

The pixie grinned and sat on the top of my right ear. This way I could hear him, but he didn't have to fly around. He was getting tired.

I sloppily made the bed and set Dirk on top of it. He took up almost the entire thing.

"Quite imposing," said the pixie. He sounded faintly out of breath. I took him from my ear and laid him gently by the shark.

"Yes, he is, isn't he?" Really, he was perfect.

"I'm quite certain he'll keep those nightmares away," the pixie said, patting Dirk's sharky head. This was especially sweet, considering that the pixie had no idea what a nightmare was. They never slept, not when they were just allotted one day. There was too much to do and see.

I lay down next to Dirk and the pixie. "So tell me," I said, pushing his hair back with one finger. He seemed to enjoy this and leaned into it. "Are you happy with your life?"

He seemed surprised. "Why, of course! What a wonderful existence! I opened my eyes and there you were, and we've never left each other's side." He smiled at me fondly. "I'm so very happy that I got to spend my entire life with you. How many people get to say—"

He never finished. His time had run out.

Disposing of pixies was never easy. I used to pick them up with a tissue or the dustpan and toss them in the outside garbage, just another routine added to my day. But lately, it's been getting harder. I picked up the pixie and set him gently in a tiny cardboard ring box. I tied it with a cheery orange ribbon and set the entire thing in the garbage.

Tomorrow would be a new day and a new pixie. Already I could see the beginning of a blue and green pearly pixie egg forming in the corner of the window frame. I wondered what this pixie would look like, if she'd have long pink hair or if he'd be afraid of spiders. I wondered if I'd miss his entire formative years when I went out to get the newspaper, or if she'd be fascinated with Dirk the Hammerhead, and whether he would develop a crush on Judge Judy while watching TV. I wondered if he would die peacefully like my little pixie tonight did, or if she would just drop to the ground mid-flight, like so many others.

I wondered what it would be like to have the same friend always be by my side, your whole life long.

I wrapped my arms around Dirk, turned my face into his gray fur, and waited for the nightmares.

AVA

She knew that she was disappearing, that much was certain. It wasn't the same as dying, not quite, and so she naturally treated it in the manner that it required.

Ava slipped her pictures out of the frames at her mother's house. She crept quietly into the homes of her friends and old lovers and did the same. Her first boyfriend still had her senior year picture in a shoebox with a few love notes from her and the girl that he had cheated on her with. She burned those, too, for good measure.

She ceased to talk those last few weeks, because she heard once that sound never disappears but bounces off the planets, deep in space, forever and ever. She wanted the sound of her voice to fade away so gradually that nobody would miss her. She erased her name out of everybody's letters, their conversations, their minds.

It took some time, but she eventually managed to erase her face from their memories as well. Zack B., the boy who sat next to her in English for four years straight, was the hardest. This was surprising, since they were never really close friends, not in all that time, but his brain had wrapped around her blonde hair and he refused to let her go. It was kind of sweet, actually, but in time she won out.

Her hair grew lighter and lighter. She forgot to eat and her body thinned and her stomach stuck against the bones in her back. When she gazed at the world around her, the color drained out of her eyes until they were perfectly clear.

It was a Wednesday, her last day. She hadn't worn any jewelry in weeks; it was too heavy and she wanted to be weightless. She breathed in once, twice, three times; the wind fluttered the curtains and there was a soft sound, a rustle of white beach sand that fell chiming to the floor, particles that were too small to be anything of consequence, to be anything at all.

She Called Him Sky

There was a boy. And there was a girl. Many stories begin this way.

The boy was a sad, beautiful boy. He carried something small and bruised in his hands. The boy stumbled through the forest, tripping in the ivy and knocking his head against the trees. He staggered through the desert, falling down and walking on his knees. He crawled through the artic cold, blowing on the slight, battered thing in his hands.

One day the boy met the girl.

She was passing through the cornfields when she saw something pale amidst the green. She stepped closer, and realized it was a white hand, palm upward. The hand belonged to an arm, and the arm attached to a very-much-asleep boy. His other hand was fisted tightly.

"Boy," she said, and pulled on his outstretched hand until his eyes flew open. They were black as night with no white at all and shone as though he were crying. His oil slick eyes roamed around a bit wildly until they landed on the tan face of the girl.

"Hello," she said, and studied him seriously. Then she smiled. "I think you could use some help."

She took the boy home, gave him a bath, and gave him a name. She called him Sky because he always looked so sad, like the stars look sad. She thought of how the moon was always alone, never invited to tea, an eerily beautiful voyeur. Sky was just the right name.

The girl didn't have a name herself, and it didn't matter because the boy couldn't speak. He just held whatever it was tightly in his hand, careful never to drop it.

"May I see what it is?" she asked him, and after thinking it over, he slowly opened his fingers.

It was a heart made out of red crystal, only now it was fissured and tender to the touch. The fire inside the heart had almost gone out, and even as the girl watched, a small bit of it crumbled to dust and fell away.

"Oh," said the girl. She looked at the boy. "Sky," she said, "I might be able to fix this. It could take me a while. May I try?"

He watched her with his strange eyes and then he nodded. The girl gingerly took the heart into her warm hands.

"I will take it into my shop where it will be safe. I will bring it back to you when the moon is the same shape it is now. All right?"

Again the boy nodded. The girl held the heart close to her chest and ran back to her shop. She carefully set the heart on a scrap of blue fabric, and surveyed her many tools. Then she got to work.

Every evening she worked on repairing the red crystal heart, and every day she spent time with the boy. He pointed at the birds and she told him their names. He pointed at the water and she showed him how to wash. He pointed at the honey-haired girl who lived down the lane, and the girl's eyes stung a bit.

"Yes, she is very pretty. And very, very kind. Her name is

Asphodel, which is a type of lily. Me? I am not called anything." She smiled at the boy. "The sun is going down. I shall leave now to work on your heart."

She worked so hard that she didn't see the sun for days, but the time had come. The moon was fat and heavy in the sky. The boy's eyes pulled away from Asphodel's home long enough to see that the girl was walking toward him, something carefully cupped in her hands.

The heart was beautiful, shiny and full of burning life. The fissures had mended, the broken edges had been smoothed and polished. He held his hands out for it, and the girl let her fingers linger on his for a second when she passed it to him. Then she pulled them away.

"It is good, Sky. It is strong and able to withstand much, I think." She watched his liquid eyes drift toward Asphodel, a compass to True North. Her lips turned upward. "I believe it is strong enough to survive if you give it to Asphodel. I think that you should try."

He looked at her then, gave her a brotherly kiss and sprang to his feet. His footsteps were whispers.

The girl picked her way through the flowers on the way back to the shop, but she never made it. She fell, silently, and her hand found its way inside her shirt to the hole where her plump, healthy heart had been. The boy's small ragged heart was still wrapped in fabric on her table, resistant to filler, resistant to files. Buffing didn't warm it, fires didn't fuse it. Sometimes, something so broken can only be replaced.

The flowers were soft. There was no sound.

MOVING TO LAS VEGAS: A PERSONAL ESSAY

When Niko was three years old, our lives changed. It changed in small ways. It changed drastically.

Luke got a job working in Las Vegas. While both Luke and I have enjoyed Vegas in the past, neither of us ever wanted to live here. But a job is a job, and a job with good medical insurance is the Holy Grail when you rack up the type of hospital bills that we do.

Saying goodbye has never been so difficult, and I've said my share of goodbyes. I wander down the halls of the children's hospital and my eyes tear up. This is the place of Niko's childhood. We pet the animal statues on every visit. While we spent time in parks and grocery stores, it seemed the majority of Niko's young life has been spent here. I both love and loath this place. It is conflicting.

We say goodbye to the people who brought us dinners and cheerful cards. We hug friends who visited Niko when he was full of tubes, and who hadn't been horrified when he vomited on their shoes. They knew him before the diagnosis. Even more importantly, they had stuck around with him afterward.

As we drive away from our home, I try to convince myself that this is a happy occasion. The tears tell me otherwise.

The 115-degree Las Vegas weather is a shock. Niko can't adjust to the change in environment. It's impossible to take him outside. We can't go anywhere in the stroller, and this especially affects us. Our daily walks saved us while we were in Seattle, but now we are trapped inside of our tiny apartment.

Luke's new job has the dreaded "busy season." His work hours stretch out longer and longer. He is working several hours a day every day during the summer without his usual time off. I have a sad, displaced child and no way to sooth him. How can I? I'm equally as lonely.

Moving to a new town means that we must introduce Niko as a child with special needs. These people didn't know him before the diagnosis; he came to them already pre-labeled. I don't know quite how to handle this. It has never happened to us before.

Do I explain that he has Williams Syndrome? Will people understand him more if they are aware of his struggles? Do I keep it to myself? The older that Niko becomes, the more glaring the gap is between his abilities and those of a typical child. It is easy to tell that "something is wrong," but how much more do people need to know?

I shouldn't have worried about it. We spend over a year in Las Vegas without any friends at all. Nobody cares about Williams Syndrome. There is nobody to call on the phone, nobody to go shopping with. Vegas is a transient town where people move in and out so quickly that it doesn't seem worth the effort of making friendships. Depression hits hard.

"How was work today, Luke?"

"Long. How was your day? Why are you crying?"

I wish I could convey the struggle, but I can't. I know that many of you understand exactly what I'm saying even if I don't have the words. You know. We know.

This is not what life is about. Life is about joy and glitter and butterflies. We focus on these things even if there is a grim iron skeleton underneath. Without hope, we cease to be. I had ceased to be shortly after moving to this new city of anonymity. I faded away until there was nothing left.

Enough.

One day I wake up and decide that Luke needs a wife. Niko needs a mother, and I deserve to have my needs met, too. I turn on the computer and sign up for an online writing course from the local university. I also decide that I am going to write my first novel. This is frightening and new. My fingers literally tremble over the keyboard as I type, but in this act, I find a way to ground myself. I kick my way out of the tangled sheets of depression, at least for a while.

Luke becomes an able provider. Niko continues to grow and thrive. And I become a writer.

BIG MAN BEN

He was almost seventeen, but not quite. She was nearly ten years older, but again, not quite.

He was out in the park, doing clumsy boy things with his clumsy man-boy body. Riding bikes. Chasing squirrels. Searching the shrubbery for things that had fallen out of other people's coat pockets, like pocketknives and pictures of old girlfriends.

She was bundled up in a lavender coat, her legs pulled up to her chest against the cold. A tiny thing with dark hair and large, expressive brown eyes. Her eyes were always brimming, but he didn't know that yet; didn't know anything yet.

He looked at her. Once. Twice. Pretended he was looking anywhere but there. Stared at her hard. Turned his head her way every four or five minutes. Every thirty seconds.

"Excuse me," she said. Her voice, like the rest of her, was frail. He was afraid the condensation from her breath would freeze and do her in. She'd fall to the ground and he'd try and rub the warmth back into her hands, breathe life into her body.

"Yes, ma'am?"

"Please don't call me 'ma'am'. I'm not old enough for that yet."

"Yes, ma'am."

He wandered over to her, too casually. Tripped. Caught himself and skulked the rest of the way to the bench in embarrassment. He hovered a few feet away.

"Do I frighten you?" she asked.

He puffed out his chest, yawned. "Nothing scares me. Ma'am."

She smiled then, and something inside his chest broke. It reminded him of when the barn cat had kittens once. Fragile things, balls of puff with miniature bones inside. The fur seemed soft enough to keep them safe, but they were still bags of bones, sacks of fragility like everything else.

This kitten girl stared up at him from inside her soft lavender coat. "Will you sit with me for a while?"

"Why?"

"I don't want to be alone," she said. Such a simple thing. So honest. He had no idea of the implication. He was just a boy.

He sat. She smiled. He was afraid he was breathing too hard. Held his breath. Coughed it out. Breathed in carefully through his nose.

"You don't need to be so afraid," she said. She was whispering now, like they were an invisible secret. The world faded and so did they.

"Told you. I'm not scared of anything." Said with a bit of pomp, but a lot of earnestness.

Her eyes brimmed, but he wasn't looking, didn't know what to be on the lookout for.

"I am," she said.

Her name was Angelica. Fitting, he thought. She was so full of goodness that she glowed. He expected wings to unfold from her back then and there.

She laughed when he said this. His ears burned, but in pleasure. She didn't laugh meanly like most girls, but was genuinely delighted.

"Oh, you sweet, silly boy," she said, and smiled directly into his eyes. "Aren't you delightful? You are. You're charming. What is your name?"

His name was Ben. Something simple, something nondescript. Nothing like Angelica.

"Ben is a wonderful name," she said adamantly. She looked at him out of the corner of her eyes, summing him up. His ears burned again. This time it was more uncomfortable.

"Yes, Ben is a fine name." She nodded to herself. "It's strong and straight and firm. I could very much grow to like a man named Ben. And you will be a man one day, you know. A fine man, if your name has anything to do with it."

"I'm a man now," Ben told her. His voice squeaked for the first time in a long time, and it embarrassed him, made him angry.

She patted his hand, but it wasn't at all condescending. "No, you're not a man yet, Ben. Almost, but not quite." He bristled at this, but she shook her head. "Don't be in such a rush to grow up. Look at you now. Your eyes are clear; your hair is too long. You don't know whether to smile or be angry at the things that I say. You're beautiful. You're simply beautiful."

Ben's eyes rolled in his head. Beautiful? Him? Plain, sturdy Ben? He wanted to laugh. He wanted to hit her for making fun of him. He wanted to believe she was telling the truth.

She sighed then, and it was weary. The force of her sorrow fatigued him. He couldn't carry its weight on his adolescent shoulders. It was the sigh of a woman, not somebody caught between childhood and adulthood like himself.

"Hmm," he said under his breath. He shifted uncomfortably.

"What is it?" she asked. She looked hurt, or maybe a little afraid. He couldn't tell such things yet.

"You sound like...your thoughts are very heavy. It does not sound easy to be an adult."

It was a lot of words for Ben. A lot to string together. A lot of thinking that went into the intent behind them.

"It isn't easy, sometimes. When I was a girl, things were so much more...I used to live then, I think."

"You don't live now?"

She shook her head, her hair falling around her cheeks like snow. "I survive."

Ben wiggled his big toes, felt the canvas of the shoe give way on his right foot. He'd been worrying at that particular hole for the better part of the day. There was something satisfying about making the hole bigger and bigger. It was like tearing apart a heart. Silencing a crying baby.

Angelica turned to face him then and the abruptness of her movement made him jump.

"Ben, I like you very much. There's something about you that is just so honest and...you ground me. Or at least I think that you could. Does this sound crazy? Do you understand what I'm saying?"

He nodded, but he wasn't really sure. She liked him? Really? She had spent ten minutes sitting on a park bench with a stranger and she actually enjoyed his company? She was beautiful. She was broken inside somehow, he knew it, but the strength of her suffering made her shine. He wished he had somebody to tell, somebody who'd disbelieve him at first, but then would slowly realize he was telling the truth. "No way!" this imaginary friend would yell, and would punch Ben excitedly in the shoulder. "No way!" But there was no such friend, so Ben chewed his lip in silence.

Angelica's brows drew up. She looked away. "I'm sorry. I'm being very forward, and I'm probably making you uncomfortable. Please forget that I..."

She tried to stand and Ben reached for her hand automatically. She stopped and stared at her gloved fingers in his bare ones. He jerked his hand away. Clenched his fists. Tentatively reached out for hers again, watching her closely to see if she'd scream and run away.

She didn't. He wanted to close his eyes and bask in her smile. A lizard on a rock. A boy with a crush.

"Ah," she breathed. He leaned in closer to hear her. "This could be something beautiful. Something amazing."

She wrapped her fingers around his, and they were surprisingly strong.

A ngelica had a husband. This changed everything.

"No, it doesn't," she insisted. It was their third meeting on the park bench. She leaned her head on Ben's shoulder and ran her finger down his arm like she owned it. Perhaps she did. "This doesn't change a thing."

Ben wanted to look at her, wanted to stare her down the way a man should. But he wasn't a man, not yet, and it had never seemed more painfully obvious than it did now. A man would shake his head defiantly and stride away. Ben wanted to cry.

"My good boy," she said, and nuzzled her face into his neck. Ben wondered what he smelled like to her. Like soap and acne medicine, most likely. The smell of a boy. The smell of a child. He pulled away.

Angelica's eyes started to get wet, and Ben looked down at his shoes. His big toe had emerged the victor, and he could see a white swath of sock. How terrible he must look to her now. A gangly youth in disrepair. He stood up.

"No, don't!" Angelica screamed, and grabbed at his arm with both hands. Ben swayed in indecision, a bit shocked by her reaction. Angelica buried her face into his sleeve and sobbed.

"Don't go," she cried. "I don't know what I'll do if you go."

Ben stood for a long while, not knowing what to do. A jogger ran past, and cast Ben a commiserating glance. "Women," it said. "Always so emotional. What's a man to do?"

A man. A man stays, Ben thought, and he sat back down, put his arms around her awkwardly.

"There there," he said. He had heard that this was the thing to say to a crying woman, but he had no idea why. "There there."

It worked. He had found the magic words, and as Angelica's tears dried to a sniffle, he repeated these wonderful words until they had become a mantra. "There there, Angelica," he said. "There there, Angie. There there, my girl. My love." He tried the endearments on. Did they fit? Would they hang on her thin frame? Would one of them truly make her his?

Angelica smiled then, into the front of his coat. He could hear it in her voice. "Call me anything. Call me everything. I like it all."

Did she?

"Do you?"

There was something behind her eyes, something watchful and weary. It sighed and gave itself over, disappeared. "I do."

"What...does your husband call you?"

He was trying to wrap his head around it. A husband. A man she told secrets to and ate dinner with and made love to. Ben felt lonely. The muscles in his left arm jerked and then quieted.

She watched his face carefully. "He doesn't call me anything, anymore. I'm just a warm body. I'm furniture. I'm art."

She was beautiful. She could be hung from the walls like a Picasso, he believed it. She would dress up the room simply by being there.

"You're the best kind of art," he said. He blushed. He looked at the trees.

"Ben." Her voice was close to his ear. He scuffed his shoe against the ground. "Ben, I'm going to tell you flat out. I'm never going to sleep with you. Never. I won't betray my husband that way." He was silent, thinking. Angelica started moving every part of her body at once, like a bird. A snake. Something that was dying a piece at a time. "Ben? Does this change things?"

She wanted him to say that it didn't, he could tell. But he had a lot to think about. A husband? Betraying? Did that mean that—?

"—you'll never be mine," he said. He said it very quietly, but she heard. She kissed the tender spot beneath his ear.

"No," she said. Her voice sounded very sad. "I won't."

"You belong to him."

She shook her head fiercely. "I don't belong to anyone."

She didn't make the next two meetings. But she had left a note taped to the underside of the bench. He'd waited quietly for her, and then dropped to his hands and knees, looking for something that might explain her absence. The note led him on a scavenger hunt, and at the end he opened a present wrapped in red paper. There was a new pair of sneakers inside. Angelica had drawn a heart on the underside of each tongue. This made Ben feel pretty good.

"What are you good at, Ben?" she asked him one day. He wasn't sure what to say.

"Math, I guess. And I like taking things apart. I like seeing how they work, and putting them back together."

"Like cars and stuff?"

He shrugged. "Sure. I work on cars."

The winter had ended, and spring bathed the park in flowers. Angelica wore a simple white daisy in her hair. Ben wondered if her husband had given it to her.

Angelica turned to face him, her eyes wide. She gripped his hands, and he was shocked at how cold they were. He rubbed them to warm them. It felt natural.

"We're moving," she said.

Ben's hands stopped mid-rub. "What?"

Angelica's pink mouth trembled at the corners. "We're moving. Soon. In about a month."

"Where?"

"Michigan."

He started to ask why, but it didn't matter. How could she leave him like that? Was this hard for her?

"Are you going to miss me at all?" he asked.

Her eyes brightened. "I'm going to die without you," she said. Ben was pleased.

"Where are you in school?" she asked.

Ben reeled at the change of subject. "Uh, one more year. I'm a junior."

A junior. And she was an adult. With a husband, a husband whose name she wouldn't tell him, who was taking her somewhere far away. And he was still in high school, eating lunch in the cafeteria and learning about biology. Pathetic.

"Move with me, Ben. Finish your senior year in Michigan."

He stared at her. She stared back.

"You want me to come with you?"

"I've thought it all out! You'll transfer to a different school. Or you can get your GED with night classes."

"You want me to drop out of school?"

She was getting angry now. "No! I said get your GED! You could be a mechanic, Ben. You like cars. There are classes that will show you how to...I'll pay. I'll pay the deposit on your apartment, and for your mechanic courses. I can't live without you, don't you understand? If you don't come with me, I don't know what I'll do!"

She was crying again, but he was too numb to effectively calm her.

"But my mom—" he began. Angelica stood up and ran away. It wouldn't be the last time, but it was certainly the first, and it hit him like a punch to the gut. She ran. She ran. This could be the last time that he saw her. Ever.

He stood up. "I'll do it!" he screamed. His family, his senior year, it didn't matter. Angelica mattered. Being her Big Ben mattered. He'd work as a mechanic during the day and throw his greasy arms around her every night, if that's what she wanted. He'd do it. He'd do anything.

His mother didn't understand.

"Why would you want to move all the way to Michigan? What could possibly be out there for you?"

"I want to try something different, Ma. I'm bored here."

"You wouldn't be bored if you did a few more chores."

This was a lie. Ben was becoming a man, and men didn't neglect the things that needed doing around the house. He had checked a book out of the library on home repairs. He'd fixed the leaky toilet and then put the closet doors back on their tracks. His mother had been very pleased.

But she sure wasn't pleased now. "And dropping out of school? Are you crazy?"

"Ma, technically it isn't dropping out. I'd get—"

She wouldn't be dissuaded. "You think you're going to get out to some new town, get all settled in, and decide to start going back to school? Think you can handle a job and school at the same time? It's not going to happen, Ben. In fact—" Her eyes widened in horror. "This isn't about a girl, now, is it? Is some girl going to Michigan? Is that what happened?"

Ben's ears reddened. "Mom, it doesn't have anything to do—"

She said that she didn't believe him, that Ben was a terrible liar. And she told him that he had always been a terrible son. A selfish, lazy thing who spent all of his time wandering around at the park when he should have been home helping his hardworking mother. A dimwitted boy who thought more about some girl than he did his own family...

Ben's intention had been to move to Lowell, Michigan, a month or two after Angelica did. As it happened, he moved out that very night. He didn't have a choice.

"What have I done to you?" Angelica asked him. Her lips trembled, but Ben didn't look away.

"You haven't done a thing to me, Ang. You make me happy."

"What kind of happiness can you have?" *With me.* He heard the words although she didn't speak them.

"What kind of happiness could I have without you?"

She closed her eyes, leaned her head against his shoulder, and cried. His coat dampened with her tears, but instead of irritating or embarrassing him, it made him feel stalwart and useful. Caring. Her good, confident Ben.

"I hate this town, Ben. I hate it so much! And you shouldn't be here. You should be in school, and dating...dating girls..." Her pretty mouth twisted around the words, and this, too, made Ben happy.

"Do you wish that I hadn't come after you?" he asked. His eyes were following a bird as it flew high above the park. Their new park. It seemed they were forever destined to sit companionably side by side on sleepy park benches.

"Yes. No. I'm glad, but only for my sake. I'm selfish, and I want you here for me, for my sake, but for you..."

He wanted to kiss her. In any other world that would be the correct thing to do. He'd take her in his arms and kiss her doubts away. He'd kiss his soul into hers. He'd kiss her husband out of their lives.

But no. There were rules. No kissing and no "I love yous," and never knowing her husband's name. He mustn't follow her home. She wouldn't give him her phone number. They communicated through hidden notes in trees like children, and occasionally a short "Meet me tomorrow" phone call that she'd make. It was like a game. It was playing house. It was capture the flag.

"Do you want to?" she asked him. Ben was caught off guard.

"Do I want to what?"

"Date other girls. Because you can. If you want to."

It was a test. She was testing him. She was trying to keep her voice steady, but she wasn't doing a very good job of it. She was staring at the tiny nick on his face where he had cut himself shaving because she couldn't look him directly in the eyes. Ben was picking up on this sort of thing.

He put his arms around her, liking the way that she folded into them. He kissed her hair.

"I told you never to kiss me," she said. Her voice was muffled by his coat.

"I'm not kissing you. This isn't real." He kissed her hair again and rested his cheek on the top of her head. "I don't want other girls, okay? I want you. I only want you." He glanced down at his watch. "I have to go to class. Are you going to be all right?"

She nodded, and he held her for a few extra seconds before he grudgingly pulled away. He smiled at her. She smiled back. All was right with the world.

He didn't go to the GED ceremony. Angelica couldn't come, naturally, and it was too expensive for his mother to fly out. But he received a pair of nice cufflinks in the mail, and his mother called him that night.

"Oh, honey, I'm so proud of you! You worked hard and finished up so quickly! Are you having a good time?"

Yes, it was good, it was lovely, and he was doing just fine. Yes, eating well enough. Yes, he had friends.

"Anybody special in your life?"

"Just you, Mom."

The harsh words had long since been forgotten. Ben could see how his sudden desire to move had hurt her, could see that deep inside her body she was just a girl. Just like Angelica was a girl.

"I love you, Mom."

"I love you, too, Benny."

"Nobody calls me Benny anymore."

"No, I suppose that they don't."

Ben saved up his money to buy a shirt nice enough to wear cufflinks with. He showed up at the park one day looking fine and dandy.

Angelica was sitting on a bench close to theirs, her head resting on the shoulder of another man.

Ben stood there awkwardly. He wanted to run. He wanted to knock the man over and steal Angelica away. Was he the husband? Another lover? Did she keep a stable of them?

He decided that continuing on would be less conspicuous than standing there, staring. He subtly summed up the fellow as he walked past. Neat, well dressed. About 40 or so, fairly grizzled. His arm fell about Angelica in a way that said possession. Ah, her husband.

You'll never own her, Ben thought, and nodded politely as he passed. Angelica's husband nodded back. Angelica stared resolutely at the ground, but he saw her lips tighten slightly.

"You were nervous," he said to her several weeks later. She hadn't dared see him for that long.

"Extremely nervous. You have no idea how nervous. And you walked by like...didn't it bother you at all?"

Ben almost laughed, but she wouldn't like that. But he smiled, and he couldn't help it. He didn't want to.

"I didn't like seeing you with him. He looks too serious."

She sighed. Ben had heard that sound many times, but it was uniquely hers. Her sound. When he'd think of her in the future, he'd think of that sigh and the things that it told him, when he was old enough to hear.

"He is very serious. But he's a good man, and I won't have you saying anything disparaging about him."

Ben frowned. "When have I ever, Ang? I never have." He stood up. "I have to go."

She was surprised. He could read it on her face, in her eyes. She was hurt, too, and in a strange way it made him feel good. Little boys couldn't hurt a woman, but a man could.

"So soon?" she asked him.

"I think it's best."

She reached her soft fingers toward him, but he hurried away. The steady thump of his boots were soothing. They reminded him of home.

Ben turned 21 in Oklahoma. His mother called and told him that she was proud of him, that she had always been proud of him. She reminded him how he had always loved a parade as a kid and used to follow the clowns down the street on his tricycle. She cried. She laughed. Her voice was wistful and soft and even a little angry by turns. She was alone. She was forgotten.

Angelica snuggled into his arms and nuzzled her nose into his neck.

"Happy birthday, baby," she said.

"Thanks, Ang."

She had bought him a gold watch. Impractical; he couldn't wear it at work because it would be covered with grease, but it was still beautiful. She had even had it inscribed. *For my lovely Big Ben. You're everything I ever wanted.*

"Ben?"

"Hm?"

"Why do you put up with me? With all of this? All of the moving and meeting on park benches?"

Because he loved her. He wanted to tell her, but it broke the rules.

She watched him expectantly.

"You know why, Angelica."

She bit her lip, and he knew that she'd be dashing at her eyes soon, blinking hard to keep the tears from running mascara down her face.

"Ben, I can never—"

"Shh. I know."

She could never. It was her mantra. She clung to it because somehow it made everything all right in her mind. She could never love him. She could never kiss him. She could never be his. This wasn't betrayal, because it was nothing.

Every night he fell asleep wondering what her lips would feel like. Would he recognize their taste? Would they somehow be familiar, like something he had long forgotten? Sometimes he was angry at the way his life was turning out. It was like being married to a ghost. Other times he was grateful he had managed to wrap his arms around something so ephemeral.

He rubbed his cheek against her hair. "You can never," he said. "But I can always."

"I'm going to have a baby, Ben. I'm going to be a mother."

He forgot how to breathe. He exhaled and then kept right on going. His body deflated and faded like a week-old birthday balloon.

"Ben? Are you all right?"

He wasn't all right. He wasn't all right. He was insanely jealous. He wanted to put his hand on her stomach and will the baby away. His Angelica, trapped by another man's child. Now she could never leave. She was not art anymore, but had become something functional. He hated it. He despised this baby.

"I'm so happy, Ben! Can you believe it?" She hugged him. "Finally I won't be so alone." She ignored the rigidness in his body, and ran her nose along his ear. "I waited until today to tell you. Happy birthday."

The baby never stopped fussing. Angelica seldom showed up at the park anymore, and when she did, she looked wild.

"Take him, will you?" she said, shoving Baby Ethan into his arms. "I can't have him pawing at me anymore today." She leaned back on the bench and shook her dark hair out of her eyes. "All I want to do is sleep. Who knew this would be so awful?"

The baby looked at Ben and sobbed. Ben turned him away so that he could see the people strolling in the park, and rocked him gently. He'd learned how to do this in the last few months.

"He's just a little kid, Ang. You need to be patient."

Angelica sat up and glared at him. "How dare you tell me how I need to be? You have no right! You're just a boy yourself!"

Ben looked at her calmly. "No, I am not a boy. I haven't been a boy for quite a while, but I don't think that you've noticed." He took in her tangled hair and the dark circles around her eyes. She had tiny lines appearing around her mouth. "And you're not a girl anymore, Angelica. This baby is your responsibility, not mine. You need to own up to him." Ben set Baby Ethan gently on her lap, but she refused to put her arms around him.

"I don't want him anymore. I don't want anything to do with him."

Ben stood up, taking the boy with him. His mouth felt ugly.

"Angelica," he said, and the baby howled. He softened his tone, but it wasn't for the woman's benefit. "I'm tired of it. I'm tired of the way that you treat everybody. You don't just get tired of somebody and give them back!"

He was yelling now, and the baby was screaming again. Heads turned toward him, and he tried to hand Baby Ethan to her again. Again, she refused, her eyes narrow and dangerous. Ben knew the look, knew what she wanted him to do. *I'm sorry, baby. I didn't mean it, baby. I can't live without you, baby.* He'd done it before.

"One day," he said, and his voice shook. He was sixteen again, a too-tall boy with too-long hair and humiliating holes in his sneakers. "One day you're going to tire of me the way that you tired of your husband. And what am I going to do then?"

Her eyes broke. He kissed Baby Ethan on the top of his head, and this time when he handed the baby back, she took him.

Baby Ethan had become Little Boy Ethan. He learned to walk by the ocean. He learned to talk in the desert.

"It is the way of it," she told him. "It's just how it is."

Ben held Little Boy Ethan on his lap. Ethan squirmed for a few minutes, but soon settled. He seemed to like Uncle Ben.

"How do you like the new place?" Angelica asked him. She had cut her dark hair into a short, serviceable cut. Still beautiful, yes, but different. Ben ran his fingers through it, and the sharp ends of her hair bit into his fingers.

"It's all right," he said. He shrugged. "I don't really get attached anymore, you know. One place is as good as another." *A car is a car,* he thought. *A mechanic is a mechanic.*

"Ben, are you happy?" she asked. She turned to look at him fully, her warm eyes threatening tears. How charming that used to be, back when he was young, before he was tired. Sometimes it charmed him still.

"I'm happy," he said, and smiled at her. When she smiled back, he realized that he spoke the truth. "Wherever you are, that's where I want to be, Ang. I don't mind moving. It's worth it."

Little Boy Ethan reached up and patted Ben's stubbled chin.

"How about you?" Ben asked the boy. "Are you happy?"

"Happy," he agreed, and Ben smiled.

"See?" he said, and grinned at Angelica. "You make the world ha—what's wrong?"

Her eyes were spilling tears, but Ben knew right away that these were tears that he had never seen before, and he thought that he had seen them all. He clutched Little Boy Ethan closer to him. These were hard tears, heavy tears. They were luminous with seriousness and a hint of impending tragedy. He feared these tears.

"Angelica, tell me what's wrong."

She didn't say, but her eyes darted to her son. Ben held him closer.

"What is it? Is there something wrong with Ethan? Tell me!"

She didn't think he could handle it. She didn't think his shoulders were broad enough to bear whatever it is that they had to bear. After all of these years, didn't she know? He could do anything for her. He would do *everything* for her.

Ethan squirmed from Ben's grasp and fell onto the grass. Ben pulled Angelica into his lap with a desperate force that surprised both of them. He put his hands on either side of her face and made her look at him.

"This is different," he said.

Her eyes skittered away but the tone of his voice pulled them back to him.

"Ang. Tell me what's wrong."

Ethan was laughing and rolling on the ground. Angelica started sobbing, a deep sound that made Ben want to cover his ears. His mother made that sound when she found out that his father was never coming home. Ben felt like vomiting.

He threw his arms around her and pulled her face to his shoulder. She didn't say anything more that evening, but she cried until her voice was hoarse and her body trembled. Ben held a woman that seemed like a stranger, and watched her child play at his feet.

Angelica wiped her eyes on her sleeve and left with Ethan, Ben stayed for a long time, looking at the stars.

They started radiation quickly; there was no choice. They actually had another move coming up, but postponed it until Angelica was feeling better. Ben waited at the park bench night after night. He held a tiny stuffed angora bunny in his hands. It had charming button eyes that would make Ang smile. If she ever showed up.

Fall hit early and it hit hard. Ben wrapped himself in thicker sweaters and scarves in order to keep watch on the bench. He was sure it was too cold for her to come, too brutal on her frail body. Ethan would catch a cold. He knew this. They should be inside their warm house where that man, her husband, could dote on them. At least, he'd better be doting on them.

Ben realized that he was squeezing the rabbit too hard. He had bent the ears, and it gave the rabbit a sad, listless appearance. Ben spent the next two hours in the cold, straightening and restraightening them. He didn't care if anybody saw him crying.

Halloween. Thanksgiving. Christmas. The rabbit now sat at home on his dresser, but Ben still came faithfully. He thought about Ethan playing under the Christmas tree. Would his mother be there? Or had she...

He didn't want to think about it. His manager's wife baked him cookies for the holidays, and he threw them out. He didn't want to look at her sultry eyes or the way that she always crossed her legs whenever he walked by. At the garage's New Year's party, she pinned him against the back room wall and whispered some rather creative suggestions. He thought of Angelica's brown eyes, and shuddered. He quit. He was young; he could get another job. He could move wherever he wanted to. Somewhere new. Somewhere without memories. On Valentine's Day he found himself at the airport, on a plane. He bought a ticket for the first flight out, and that evening he was living in Portland, Oregon. The gritty rain settled him.

He started calling his mom weekly. He entertained the idea of driving down to see her and help out around the apartment. He took a break from working on cars and worked in a music store instead. He had forgotten how much he liked to listen to the guitar, how he learned the lyrics after only hearing them once. His heart broke for Angelica, but without so much as a last name, he could never track her down. He could never find out what had happened, or where she was buried, or where Ethan would be. Ethan was too young to remember him, anyway. And what would he matter to that little boy? He was only a strange man, an elusive entity who haunted park benches.

It was tough, but he was tough. He had learned how to take care of himself. He had learned how to be kind. There was a pretty redhead who worked at the Greek shop across the way. Her shirts were always too big and her hair was wild. He had blinked at her a few times before ducking out quickly. On Wednesday, when she handed him his gyro, she smiled at him.

In the last seven years, Ben had never smiled at another woman besides Angelica. But on this day Ben smiled back.

That night an envelope arrived. It had been sent to his old address before being forwarded to Portland. Inside was a pink piece of paper with familiar handwriting.

"Baby. Come to Tucson."

Her brown eyes dominated her face. Her thin, worn, beautiful, beautiful face. Ben stood in front of her uncertainly. She perched on the park bench like it hurt her.

"Hiya, baby," she said. "Welcome to Arizona."

His eyes scraped over her. The color of her skin and the delicate way that she held her body. She turned her face toward the sun and closed her eyes.

"Doesn't it feel wonderful to be warm?" she asked.

Ben fell to his knees in front of her, dropping his forehead to her lap.

"I thought, I thought," he repeated. It was okay for a man to cry when he realized that his life has been taken from him, or given back to him; he couldn't decide which.

"Shh," she whispered, and stroked his light hair. "Shh, my boy. My love."

Her short hair was carefully brushed and her lipstick was applied with extra care. Ben didn't know that Angelica had decided that, just this once, she would be willing to break her rules. If there was anything that she needed right now, it was to be loved. It was to be kissed by her Ben and to kiss him back in return. There was life in a kiss, and love in a kiss, and more than anything she wanted life and love, but it was not to be. Ben sobbed into her skirt just as she had sobbed into his shoulder months before. The moment came and the moment went, and Ben was fortunate enough not to realize it.

She truly could have been his.

"Ethan is in daycare," she said to him one day. She sat on Ben's lap with her arms around his neck. She wanted to feel all of him. She wanted to make sure that they were both breathing.

"Is it too difficult for you when he is home? Are you tired?"

She shrugged. "Yes and no. He always wants something. He

wants a drink or a cracker or to show me a new toy. It gets wearying. You have no idea." She stretched. "You're so lucky that you don't have children, Ben. They're just so..."

He waited, but she didn't finish. Finally he spoke.

"I want kids someday."

Angelica was surprised. "You do?"

"I do."

"But why?"

He didn't know. It's just the way that it was. To have a child who followed you around, who wanted to be with you and who wore your hat when you came home from the shop. Who wanted to see your tools and made faces when you kissed his mother at night.

"I like kids," he said simply.

Angelica snorted. "Well, you won't be getting any from me, that's for sure. Not that I can have any more after the surgery, anyway. But still."

She eyed him then, and he tried not to sigh as he recognized the look in her eye.

"Do you want kids that badly? You really want them?"

"Let's talk about it later, Ang."

It was dangerous territory that he was wading in. He rubbed her back in what was usually a comforting manner, unless she was riled. And she was riled.

"No, we will talk about this now. You really want kids? I can't give them to you." She hopped off of his lap, and Ben knew it was over now, it was over and he would have to watch her self-destruct. *When somebody faces cancer,* his doctor had told him when he had asked, *there is an emotional toll. People lose a part of themselves. They face their own mortality.* Whatever it was, it had turned angelic Angelica into something shriveled and mean. It had eaten away at her soul as well as her organs.

"Ang, I was only saying—" he began.

"I'm not enough? You want more? I can give you my heart and my soul, but you want children? *Children?* It's impossible! You won't get it from me, do you understand?"

People were staring at them. Ben wanted to shrug and duck his head. He wanted to push Angelica down and cover her mouth with his hand. But in the anger, he could see her fear, the absolute wildness pushing itself against the shadowed glass of her eyes. *I'm broken,* the fear told him. *I'm broken and I can't give you anything, not even my last name.*

"Maybe you ought to find yourself another girl, then. Somebody who is whole—" her voice cracked "—and complete and healthy. And you can start a family, and she'll be there... Oh, God, what have I done to you?" She turned and wheeled away, her hands over her face. She ran through the park toward her car, and people slowly turned their heads away.

Ben looked down at his hands. He flexed them, watching the veins ripple under the skin, seeing the strength underneath the grease he could never quite wash off. His hands were empty, as usual. More than ever, he was beginning to realize that.

She disappeared. Again. Ben didn't know what to think.

He thought about skipping their meetings. That would show her. She'd sit on the bench in the hot Arizona sun, waiting for him. For hours. She'd wait and get hot and thirsty and think he had abandoned her. She'd feel how he felt when he sat there alone. It was a lonely feeling, the worst feeling in the world.

He never missed an appointment.

It gave him time to think. Did he love her? Yes, he did. More than anything. More than his family, more than his old friends. More than school and the hope of finding a better job. When she told him about moving, a small part of him always resented it, because she would never move for him. But still he dropped everything because of her. His Angelica, his angel. How could he live without her? Would he really have a life to go back to?

One particularly windy day, he approached the bench to find a little girl sitting on it. She looked up at him worriedly.

"Are you Ben?" she asked.

He was surprised, and stood there. He shoved his hands in his pockets. He was seventeen again, a child again, back when everything first started. His chest hurt.

"Yes. I'm Ben."

The girl looked relieved. "I have something for you, and I couldn't go until you came. She said you would come. But it's so windy and the dust is in my eyes and I don't like the sound that the wind makes."

She stuffed a bent envelope into his hand and started to turn away.

"Wait," Ben said. "I don't know who you are."

The girl nearly smiled back at him, but not quite. "You're friends with my aunt Angelica. She's not feeling very good." The girl ran away then. Ben stared after her, and then his eyes slowly focused on the envelope in his hand.

He opened it, and saw a lined piece of paper with words written in an unfamiliar, bold script.

Angelica Brogan
St. Mark's Hospital
Room #301
Please Come Quickly

He stared. He stared. He read it again and again. Angelica Brogan. Beautiful. And she was in the hospital.

It was time.

His feet pounded on the ground as he ran. Real men run toward danger, not away from it, but he wasn't thinking about this at all. He was thinking about his Angelica, and her little boy, and whether or not he had time to kiss those lips for the first and last time. What would they taste like? Like death and chemo and pain, most likely. Her tears would taste the same way, but he couldn't wait to hold her and kiss the toxicity away, just as long as he could finally see her. Because life without Angelica wouldn't be any kind of life at all, and he knew it.

She lay in a hospital bed. No hair. No eyebrows. No eyelashes. She was sleeping, but her face contorted in pain. It ran underneath her nervous system. Ben stepped into the room hesitantly. He felt gangly and awkward. What if he stepped on the electrical wires? Pulled the plastic tubing from her nose and veins? He didn't know what to do with his lumbering, oversized hands and stuffed them in his pockets. Surely they would be safer there.

"You must be Ben," a voice said behind him.

Ben turned to find an ancient man standing in the doorway. His eyes were tired but kind. His face collapsed in on itself in sorrow.

Her husband.

"I'm...Ben," he said. He didn't know what else to say.

Angelica's husband reached forward to shake Ben's hand. Ben started, then fumbled his hand out of his pocket. The other man's grip was firm and strong. His wedding band flashed.

"I'm Allan," the man said. His lips tried to lift in a smile. He wasn't nearly as old as Ben had first thought. Fatigue and misery had done this to his features.

"It's...nice to meet you, Allan." It was. Ben's eyes slid over to Angelica, who moaned in her sleep. He looked back at Allan.

"It isn't long now, my boy. She's...she's ready to go, I think." His face crumpled even more, but he straightened it out. "I'm glad that you could come by. I think it's good for both of you."

Ben's world was veiled with intangibility. Angelica was dying. Her husband was shaking his hand.

"This isn't real," he whispered, and wobbled a bit.

Immediately Allan had him by the arm, guided him into a chair.

"Sit down," he said. "We don't need both of you in that hospital bed." He frowned suddenly, and aged in front of Ben's eyes once more. Ben had never felt so ashamed.

"Sir. I...Ang. Elica. Your wife. She and I never..." He couldn't finish. Allan shook his head.

"Not now."

Ben didn't know what to say. He watched Angelica's breathing. It was irregular and frightening. She had never looked so tiny.

Allan cleared his throat and looked away. "I thought you might need to say goodbye. You've meant a lot to her over the years."

Ben bit his lip. Allan stood up to leave, but Ben grabbed his sleeve.

"You don't have to go, sir. I can say goodbye with you here."

Allan made an ugly sound. "I don't want to be here for this." He gently shook his sleeve free and did a curious old-man shuffle to the door. He reached the door, but couldn't make himself pass through it. He leaned his head against the doorjamb and his hands trembled.

Ben slid out of the chair and knelt by Angelica's bed. He tried to be respectful of Allan, but seconds after patting her slender fingers, he was running his hands over her skin. Up her arms and across her butterfly eyelids. He felt her delicate skull and the hollows in her cheeks.

"I don't know what I'm going to do without you," he said. She didn't move. She couldn't respond. He rubbed his cheek against hers like a kitten starved for affection, and really, that wasn't far off. He wanted to say, "Don't leave me." He wanted to say, "I can't survive without you." He wanted to say, "I'm sorry," but, really, there wasn't anything to be said except one thing...

"I think that I will always love you. Sometimes I wish this wasn't the case."

His kiss was a tender thing, half an inch from her lips. He closed his eyes. *Goodbye.*

He turned toward Allan. "She had the utmost respect for you, sir. She wouldn't even tell me your name."

Allan's blue eyes regarded him sharply. "Do you know how I found out about you?"

Ben took a step back in surprise. "No...no, sir."

Allan's laugh was bitter and morose and baffled all at once. "We have a boy. His name is Ethan."

"Yes, sir."

Allan eyed him, but Ben returned his gaze evenly. Allan continued.

"I wanted to name him Ethan Lauran, after my father, but she wouldn't have it. She was adamant about it, which wasn't really like her at all."

It wasn't? Ben thought, but he didn't say a word.

Allan deflated. "No," he said softly. "She had a name all picked out. Benjamin Ethan."

Ben reeled again, and steadied himself on the chair.

"But..."

"That's your name. I know." Allan's mouth worked in a strange way. "And suddenly it all made sense. She didn't cry when I'd leave, anymore. She withdrew money from the bank account. It used to devastate her whenever we'd move, and then one day it was all okay. I didn't understand it. And then I didn't want to understand it." He studied Benjamin's face. "You're not what I expected."

The urge to fight flashed through Ben's body. He could stand up to this man. He was already mostly beaten. He'd fall without a sound, like flowers under snow. Angelica could be his. Her eyes would open one last time, and his smile, his warm gaze would be what she saw. How many times had he dreamed of being the one that she awoke to?

Ben took a deep, slow breath and closed his eyes.

"Sir, I...I never fully understood."

Allan blinked and took the hand that Ben offered. He shook it firmly.

"I'm sorry that things turned out this way, Ben. You seem decent enough. But sometimes life..."

Does funny things, Ben thought. *Rips your throat out. Leaves your hands empty at the end.*

Ben stuffed his hands back into his pockets. He stared at a scuff on the floor. "I'm glad that I knew your wife, and your son."

The silence pressed heavily on them. There was nothing more to say. Ben pushed his way through the door, fleeing his love and his hope as they lay dying. Angelica didn't belong to Allan. She didn't belong to Ben. And Ben was realizing that he didn't belong to her, either.

He walked down the hall, paused, but slowly continued walking. He tasted Angelica on his lips, realizing it would be for the last time. When he stepped outside of the hospital, he squinted his eyes against the sun. It illuminated. It burned.

BEAUTIFUL NOTES

"BROKEN" — This is a hint-fiction piece. "Hint Fiction" is a term coined by Robert Swartwood that has to do with hinting at a deeper story in under twenty-five words. I had a dark little tale accepted in Swartwood's *Hint Fiction* anthology, and he asked if I would be interested in writing something else for promo leading up to the anthology's release. I submitted a few pieces and was thrilled when "Broken" was chosen. It chills me. It also reminds me of a job that I held a long, long time ago. I still see those children in my nightmares.

"BLACK MARY" — Ah, "Black Mary." What to say? "Black Mary" cuts to the bone.

My friend and fellow writer Robert J. Duperre asked me to write a story for his *Gate 2* anthology. The theme was isolation and despair, and he originally pitched an idea about a woman going crazy alone on an island. It very much seemed like something I could play with, and I ended up writing about a kidnapped girl who lives alone on a farmhouse in the middle of nowhere. The only person she has to talk to is Black Mary, a rather strange friend who has secrets of her own. The eventual arrival of the Red Mary spurs the girl into action.

I choose not to explain "Black Mary." Are the Marys figments of the girl's imagination brought on by her abuse and isolation? Perhaps her mind is creating companionship. Perhaps she is haunted by the ghosts of the man's previous victims. I feel the same way about this story as I do "Music to Jump By," in that I believe you, as the reader, will correctly come to your own conclusion.

The other story behind "Black Mary" is that, at the time of writing, I was dealing with the death of two of my three triplets. They were all girls, and while I was so grateful and in love with my remaining littlest girl, I was naturally ripped apart with grief. After rereading this story later, I realized that I wrote about a surviving girl and two otherworldly (or are they?) girls who come to her aid. I think writing "Black Mary" helped me exorcise some of my grief, and I kindly thank Robert Duperre for offering me the chance to create it. Thanks, Robby D! This helped me heal.

"FLAT, FLAT WORLD" — One of my favorite stories, but also one I found difficult to place. It's a very ethereal piece about a girl who simply wants to disappear. Nothing is wrong with her life, but she finds herself fading away. It was one of my first pieces where the trees and other things of nature became sentient beings. While I was intrigued by the mysterious man who silently brushes the girl's hair, I found myself more drawn to the tree who desires to rain down flowers upon the girl. He's a thing of majesty and dignity. Very royal.

"EXTRAORDINARY BEAST" — "Extraordinary Beast" was my second attempt at the Las Vegas Killercon creative writing contest. They gave us a prompt, a few words that needed to be included, and about twenty minutes to write. I had just been looking at some of Alan Kaszowski's art, and he had a piece that reminded me of Spring-Heeled Jack, so I took the prompt, sat down, and wrote. I won first place for the second year in a row, which was an amazing feeling. I very much like the dash and the sinister intent of the male character. I do believe he'll show up elsewhere.

"THE BOY WHO HANGS THE STARS" — An experiment. A friend told me that I should write fairytales, and I told him that I didn't think I could do that. "I cannot do fairytales and horror," is what I said. But I tried my hand at it and wrote this sweet little story about two children who felt horribly isolated but figure out that a pair of wings fits as nicely around two as it does around one. This story was a game changer for me. It was one of my very first publishing credits, and it was a triumph because I got over a mental "I can't do that" type of wall. It also cemented my winged-boys and stars obsession.

"UNTIED" — This was originally named "See Jack and Jane Jump." I wanted to try my hand at a lighthearted romance, since most of my love stories have to do with the dead or dying. And what is more lighthearted than a suicidal man about to plunge from a building? Okay, so he's *almost* dead or dying. I had a wonderful professor explain that he loved the surreal and almost bizarro quality of the lecherous tie. He wondered what I was telling the reader about myself. I was flattered; I was only having fun.

"THE CONTAINER OF SORROWS" — My saving grace. I had just written *Pretty Little Dead Girls: A Novel of Murder and Whimsy* in an absolute haze of delight. Nothing had ever come as easy for me, and

I felt absolutely lost after the novel was completed. It felt like the end of a relationship, in a way. I couldn't write anything of worth for a long time, and I struggled with that. One day I was looking at my favorite piece of art by Mark Ryden. It's called "Night Visit" and it has always filled me with a quiet, beautiful horror. I sat down and wrote "The Container of Sorrows," and I was so pleased with the outcome. The white, white girl and her darling Peter, who is an important character in *Pretty Little Dead Girls,* the novel I had just finished. This story was published by *The Pedestal,* and that gained me entrance into the SFWA. "Sorrows" came at a time when I needed to know that I could fall in love with language and with my work again.

"DEADENED" — Once upon a time somewhere around 2014, I met a writer friend named Todd. I don't remember exactly why, whether it was a bet or a dare or a challenge, but we agreed to write each other into stories. I believe I was some sort of mad scientist in his tale, and he became Todd the Deadened, the UnTodded, the Moldering Todd in this story. This was back when we were new friends. Now he is my brother, and the interior designer and all-around wizard of the book you're currently holding in your hands. Thank you, my dear Todd. It was such a pleasure to kill you, but even better to have you and your family in my life.

"A PLACE OF BEAUTY" — A brief love affair with language. I wanted to write about a woman in a charming suit and hat who walked away from something somber into something better.

"MUSIC TO JUMP BY" — A story years in the making. When I was newly married, I was in our dank little apartment, soaking in the tub.

I was listening to a mix tape that I had made, and I thought, *Oh my goodness, this mix is so depressing! It's music to jump by.* The songs were kind of saying goodbye to this other, childish life I had left behind, and I was quite young and afraid of what was in store. I finished the story maybe ten years later, here in Vegas. I've been toying with the idea of drawing it out into a novel, but I'm not certain about that. While the characters have the depth to carry a novel, that would most likely mean that I would have to explain the ending, and I very much don't want to explain the ending. You, as the reader, know the ending. It may be different for every reader, but the reader's heart will tell them if he jumps, if she jumps, if she pushes him so he doesn't have to make that decision, or if they simply dance until the music goes quiet. I would also hope you would think about the soundtrack to your own life. What would it be?

"AXES" — I have a series of short stories that I write to amuse myself. I call it the "Death and Destiny" series. Death and Destiny are roommates until one day when she kicks him out for being a creepy mooch who is always late with the rent. Death drives a huge orange gas-guzzler and leaves Cheetos dust wherever he goes. In 2009 I sold a flash fiction spinoff of this series called "Lady Luck" to *Bards and Sages*. Other than that, I've kept them all for myself. Somebody suggested making them into a graphic novel series, which could be a lot of fun. It's something I'm considering.

"THE QUIET PLACES WHERE YOUR BODY GROWS" — This story hurts. "Quiet Places" is a tie-in to my Southern Gothic novel *Darling*, which was published by Black Spot Books. Azhar, in all his optimistic sorrow, shows up to comfort the main character after her child also goes missing. Azhar's character was inspired by an article I had just read about a man who goes to murder sites years later and takes pictures after the land has healed. He names them after the victims, and I found it to be very haunting and sweet and sad.

"SHOW YOUR BONES" — My first published piece. When I originally wrote it in college, it was about ten pages long. I was fed up with the beauty culture and the celebrity hype. My professor said, "You know, magazines are now publishing something called Short-Shorts." He told me to polish every word as if it were a gem. I starved the story down to its bare bones, and several years later, I sold it for twelve dollars. It was the best twelve bucks I ever made. More importantly, I was a published writer. Whenever I picture my muse, I picture the woman in this story. Sometimes she has wings, and then I believe she is truly happy.

"THE ABCs OF MURDER" — "I got really tired of murdering Billy Cords." This line just popped into my head one day, so I wrote it down. Who was Billy Cords? Why was the narrator trying to murder him? No, wait, it sounded like the narrator was *succeeding* in murdering him! How could that be? In order to answer that, I sat down and wrote "The ABCs of Murder," which was quite fun for me. Most of my stories come as a phrase or a scene, and I need to feel it out and discover what happens. It's exciting. This story won second place in *On the Premises'* contest #7, and I used the money to buy a sewing machine. Now I sew darling little skully quilts, and it gives me great joy.

"A PLACE SHIELDED FROM HORRORS" — This story is a conglomerate of some of the strange dreams I have. Toby the Tiger Shark usually follows me as I jog through town. He's quite the protector, and has a blunt, strokable nose. The Water Cat loves his water room, the singing daisies show up quite a bit, and I used to dream about that apartment with the wooden door that assembles itself every night. Welcome to the world inside my head. Sometimes it's quite terrifying, and sometimes it's a lovely place to be.

"LIKE THE STARS" — I wrote this for my first Killercon creative writing contest. We were given 20 minutes and the words "puddling," "calzone," and "night." What burdensome words! Still, I wrote. I dreamed of someone elegant and deadly, and "Like the Stars" won first place. This little story was the beginning of big things for me.

"CROSSWISE COSMOS SABOTAGE" — This is really a story about last Tuesday.

"LIFE" — One evening after the kids were asleep, I put on noise-blocking headphones. The silence was disconcertingly thick, and my heartbeat was frightening. In that silence, I wrote "Life," about a girl whose love is dying while she lies in a field with his brother. It's about mortality, and joy, and losing that joy, and trust, and mistrust, all at the same time.

"LUNA E VOLK" — We listen to a lot of Russian music in our house. One of our favorite bands has a solemn song called "Luna e Volk." It's absolutely haunting, and the singer tells of a wolf who howls at the moon with blood on its lips. The song still gives me chills after all this time. I was very inspired by the idea of a man so deeply saturated in the media that he can't truly distinguish between fantasy and reality. How would this carry over if he meets a woman so ephemeral that he thinks she must be otherworldly? I love how "Luna e Volk" turned out. It's beautifully dark.

I recorded "Luna e Volk" for episode 122 of the This is Horror podcast. Would you like to hear a story, darling? Sit beside me and I'll read to you.

"STARS" — My husband doesn't read most of my work. He likes things to be on the lighter side. "Stars" was actually something that he liked—hooray! He was my biggest cheerleader at getting this thing published. It was turned down quite a few times because the story powered along all right, but then the ending was a little too trite. After bringing it back to my writer's group, the illustrious Illiterati, they told me that the star needed to die at the end. I knew this, but I had the hardest time killing this particular darling. I wanted the star and Samson Gimble to be happy, but it wasn't their destiny. After deciding that, yes, the star must die, I rewrote the ending and submitted it to the Eric Hoffer Awards. It ended up on the short list and was included in the *Best New Writing 2012* collection, which is now sitting pretty on the shelves of my alma mater. I studied the *Best New Writing* books in college, so to be included in it now...well, that's an achievement right there. But it was still difficult to ice my little star.

"WINGS" — I dearly love this awkward boy and his cumbersome wings. While this is, in a gentle way, a tale about bullying and being shunned for differences, it's mostly a tale of love. When I look back to my school years, I think of the very, very good friends I found hidden beneath their mountains of quirks, and I'm so grateful they looked past my oddities to find out who I truly was. Life can be harsh when we're young, but when we have a little experience behind us, we discover that the things that make us odd—wings, my eyes that seem to change color, my friend's extensive My Little Pony collection—are the things that make us special. This is a story that says, "Hey, there's hope. Keep being your beautiful self and everything will work out one day."

"A House Without Corners" — This is an essay about sisters I wish I knew better, but we didn't know how to breathe together. It's a tale about a house haunted by the living.

"Sweet, Sweet Sonja T" — Before I worked for *Shock Totem*, I thought the publishing game was much more ephemeral. You shot your story into the ether and an editor magically accepted or rejected it. "Sweet, Sweet Sonja T" came about after I realized that I was sending my personal information off to total strangers, and there was a possibility that one or two of them could be complete whackjobs. That's probably the case, but the truth is, so am I, so it evens out in the end.

"Blossom Bones" — It's exactly 100 words long. I wrote it for a 100-word contest and ended up getting an honorable mention for it. This brief story gave me the chance to weave the light and the dark together. It's a terrible love story. My favorite. I have a deep love for bones and flowers, and you can now easily imagine my home décor.

"Edibility" — I remember distinctly being in a playful mood when I wrote "Edibility," and it still brings me happiness when I reread it. It is more surreal than most of my other work, I know, and although a bit bizarre, many aspects are grounded in reality. My husband saw a bobcat on an electrical line, which promptly set ablaze. I want nothing more than to pull all our grass out and have a giant flower garden instead. I love to bake star-shaped lemon cakes with johnny-jump-ups as decoration. It's strange how you can take normal everyday things, put them together, and suddenly life seems a dreamy circus.

"HEARTLESS" — This is a story that I've had in my head for quite a while. While it is, of course, a play on Eros and Psyche, which is one of my favorite tales, it's more a tentative exploration of loss. Could a woman be so consumed by her depression, so mired in her apathy that she wouldn't care if a demon came to her every night? And what of this nameless demon, who is so lonely that he is willing to cross worlds to do nothing but sleep next to a broken slip of a human woman?

The story itself is quite brief, but I'm intrigued enough by the underlying motivations of the characters that I might follow their journeys, possibly separately, and see where they end up. I'm very drawn to dark things in love.

"PIXIES DON'T GET NAMES" — I based this story on the idea of loving somebody so fiercely and intensely that it burns you alive. It came about after a spirited conversation about whether everlasting love is feasible in today's society. I adore my broken little pixie, who was horribly alone even though he never seemed to realize it. He believes in a lifetime love, as do I.

"AVA" — A short tale of a woman who knows she is going to disappear and tries to make it as painless as possible. I find that when people are fighting their most ferocious battles, they tend to pull away from the rest of us. Most likely to make it easier on us if they lose, I think, but it still hurts. I'm very afraid of losing those I love.

"She Called Him Sky" — I wrote this story for a lovely little magazine that publishes the most beautiful things. The editor requested a story, and I felt that a tale of ultimate love would fit the bill. The opening lines— "There was a boy. And there was a girl. Many stories begin this way"—was a snarky nod to the fact that most of my tales have a nameless boy and a nameless girl. I crack myself up with these inside jokes that nobody else understands. It's sad, really.

"Moving to Las Vegas: A Personal Essay" — I'm working on a memoir about my son and our experiences with Williams Syndrome and autism. This is an excerpt about moving from Seattle to Las Vegas, which was as jarring and horrific and lonely as you'd expect. But, ah, that desperation makes us strong, my loves.

"Big Man Ben" — This tale has something special. Ben tugs at my heart in a way that I can't fully describe. Perhaps it's the fact that it was based on a true story.

I was reading Dear Abby, of all things, and came across a letter that stopped my breath. A man wrote for advice, saying that he was in love with a married woman and had followed her across the United States ever since he was a young man. Now her husband was retiring, and he was afraid their affair wouldn't continue, and what was he to do? I nearly cried. It was a tale of love given and love lost. I created Ben, but I couldn't bear to leave him as a middle-aged man who had nothing of his own. So, in the most horrendous and kindest of ways, I released him. I wish him a beautiful life. He very much deserves it.

AFTERWORD

Well.

Well. As a very famous man once said, "It is finished."
Beautiful Sorrows is more than a collection of short
stories: it's a collection of my hopes and dreams. It's full of my odd
little pieces of writing, scrawled on scraps of paper and in journals
and on a faulty laptop with broken keys. It holds my tears and terrors,
and is made of whimsy and arterial spray. It contains pieces of my
soul. This book is full of people I love and maybe a few people I hate.
Beautiful Sorrows is my first published book. I held the physical copy
in my hand and thought, "At last, I am truly a writer."

John Boden, whom I call Shiney J, told you in the foreword how
Beautiful Sorrows came to be. It was very much a group effort, and
this, this Ten Year (plus one!) Anniversary Edition was once again
created through the love of my friends.

Ken, Nick, and Shiney J helped with the original publication.
Jason Sizemore and Apex graciously handed over everything I
needed to republish this book. Ken is my hero for having a backup of
all the old files, saying, "I keep everything." Yannick Bouchard, who

did the original cover and the adorable little chalk drawings that preface each story, made time to create four new drawings for this edition. Shiney J wrote a beautiful foreword that made me cry and gave me the strength to tackle this afterword. Todd Keisling created this gorgeous interior, put everything together, and kept the project organized. I couldn't have done it without him. Orion Zangara, one of the most amazing artists I've ever met, and my partner-in-crime in crafting *Pretty Little Dead Girls: A Graphic Novel of Murder and Whimsy,* created two stunning, intricate pieces of art for this edition.

This little collection is full of ephemerality, magic, and murder. She's deeply symbolic to me, and she's come home to roost. Thank you, my friends. We did it.

All my love,
Mercedes

MERCEDES M. YARDLEY is a Bram Stoker and Stabby award-winning dark fantasist who wears poisonous flowers in her hair. She writes in a lush, lyrical style about current social issues and finding love and beauty in the darkness. She authored such works as *Darling, Apocalyptic Montessa and Nuclear Lulu: A Tale of Atomic Love, Little Dead Red,* and *Love is a Crematorium.* Mercedes lives and works in Las Vegas. You can find her at MercedesMYardley.com

85077572R00142